WHO RIDES IN THE DARK?

by STEPHEN W. MEADER

Illustrated by James MacDonald

SOUTHERN SKIES
LITTLE ROCK, ARKANSAS
www.southernskies.com

Dedication

*The republication of this book is dedicated to the memory of
Frank McGehee by his friend who misses him every day,
Jerry Atchley.*

HE SWUNG THE REARING HORSE
INTO A GALLOP

FULL-PAGE ILLUSTRATIONS

WHO RIDES IN THE DARK?

ONE

A CHILL whistle of wind came over the hill and lifted the roadside dust in eddying spirals. Dan buttoned his worn jacket tighter around the emptiness of his stomach. He had been hungry and tired before in the course of his fifteen years, but never so lonely as at this moment.

With every plodding mile he was leaving farther behind him the people and places he knew. It was four days since he had shaken the dust of the flat coast country from his cowhide boots and started west toward the hills. Now even the rumbling freight wagons that had kept him company seemed to have deserted him. The turnpike lay empty in both directions and overhead the clouds had darkened ominously with a threat of rain.

He trudged upward, wondering miserably where he would sleep that night. It was just as he gained the crest of the hill and bowed into the full sweep of the autumn wind that he heard the quick beat of hooves behind him. Someone was riding fast. Too tired to be curious, the boy did not look back. He merely turned to the right and stumbled on through grass that lined the ditch at the edge of the road. Then he heard the labored breathing of the horse and the clang of shoes on broken stone, and a great black shape surged past his shoulder.

An instant later, something whirled back toward him. Instinctively Dan threw up an arm to protect his face, and the wind-blown object bounced off his elbow to roll in the ditch. It was a bell-crowned beaver hat.

Even as he stooped to pick it up he heard the clatter of hooves returning. The rider reined up beside him and he saw the tall black horse throwing spume flecks down the wind as he snorted and tossed his head. Then Dan was looking up into a pair of piercing pale gray eyes under low-growing locks of dark hair. The rider thrust an arm inside his fine blue cloak and pulled it forth again.

"Here!" he spoke suddenly, and a shining disk of metal arched through the air, clinking on a stone at Dan's feet. The man gave a short, sharp laugh. "My hat, please!" he said. He took the beaver from the boy's outstretched hand, clapped it on his head and swung the rearing horse into a gallop again.

Dan stared stupidly after him, then picked up the coin from the dust. It was a new silver dollar!

He felt more courage now as he went down the hill. Even the stinging chill of the rain that was beginning to fall could not douse his spirits. Money in his pocket! Food at the next inn! A whole dollar—just for handing a man his hat! He must be rich, that rider, thought Dan. Rich or crazy.

The rain slanted into his face harder and harder, and from the fading light he knew it would soon be dusk. He stepped under the spreading branches of an oak at the left of the road and shivered there, waiting for the force of the storm to slacken. Just as he was about to go on he heard a distant shout and the crack of a whip. The sounds came from back along the pike, beyond the crest of the hill. In a short time he saw horses' heads appear, then the swaying half-moon of a wagon canvas. There was a jingle of bells and a squeak of brake-shoes. The freighter had started down the slope.

The driver, riding the lazy-board between the two nigh wheels, called out cheerfully to Dan as his leaders drew abreast.

"A wet evenin', lad!"

The boy nodded and tried to grin. " 'Deed it is!" he answered. "Could—could you tell me how far I'll have to go to reach the next tavern?"

The wagon, with its gray canvas top drawn tight over the curved bows, was passing him now, and he splashed alongside, keeping pace with the six hurrying horses.

"Wal," said the teamster, pointing with his whip,

"that big pine down there is s'posed to be three mile from the Fox an' Stars—Skilly Bassett's place." He paused to relieve himself of a mouthful of tobacco-juice. "That's where I'm aheadin'," he continued. "Climb in over the tailboard an' git out o' the wet."

"Thank you," mumbled the boy gratefully, and in another minute he had squeezed through the narrow opening at the back of the wagon. Trying not to drip water on the cargo, he huddled down between the boxes and barrels. It was dry and warm there in the dark. He was very tired. Before the wagon had moved a hundred yards its gentle jolting had lulled him to sleep.

. . .

An hour later, when the driver's powerful hand shook his shoulder, he could not remember for a moment where he was. Then the steamy smell of horses reached him and he touched the rough side of a cask. A lantern, somewhere outside, made a moving flicker of light on the wall of canvas. He pulled himself hastily to his feet and started to clamber out.

"What ye got there?" came a querulous voice. "Some vagabone ye picked up 'long the road, I warrant!"

Dan looked out and saw a sour-faced, stoop-shouldered man in a dripping greatcoat holding the lantern high to peer at him. The boy, still only half awake, was trying to find words to tell him he had money to pay for his night's lodging, when the teamster's cheerful voice cut in.

"What?" he was saying. "This youngster? No, sirree!

He's my helper. Come, boy—let's git this team in the stable!"

Dan jumped down with alacrity and ran to the leaders' heads. As soon as his friend had uncoupled the double-tree, the boy clucked encouragingly and led the pair toward the faint radiance of the stable-door. An Irish hostler, pitching down straw from the loft, saw them and looked disgusted.

"Howly saints! Another one!" he cried. "Faith, an' we'll be tyin' 'em to trees before mornin'! Ye'll find empty stalls yonder at the end o' the row."

The long barn was dimly lighted by a single lantern, hanging on a harness-peg. Dan made his way down the line of stalls past a score of placid rumps and ushered the lead team into their quarters for the night. He was used to horses. In a jiffy he had unbuckled the tall hames with their brass bells, stripped off the heavy collars, and replaced the bridles with rope halters. As he carried the harness back he saw the teamster entering with the swing team. The wheelers followed without guidance.

Dan didn't wait for an order but began unharnessing the last pair while his friend was stabling the swing team. They were splendid horses. All big red roans, beautifully matched.

"Hm," murmured the freighter quietly. "Ye're a pretty handy lad. Better tell me a bit about yerself, 'case anybody asks questions. What do they call ye?"

"Daniel Drew," the boy replied. "I'm from Portsmouth. My father was Ebenezer Drew. He was mate on a coasting brig—sunk by a British man-o'-war in 1814, and all hands lost. My mother—" he gulped and went on with a steady voice—"my mother died a month ago. So I'm headin' west."

The teamster looked at him keenly. He was an ox of

a man, barrel-chested, with a ruddy face, clean-shaven
and kindly. "All right, Danny," he said, "I believe ye.
First off, I thought ye might be a bound-boy, runnin'
away. Not that that would ha' made any difference. I
was in the same fix myself, once. You can call me Silas.
Silas Penny is the name. I haul 'tween Bellers Falls an'
Boston, mostly. Come on—let's git the horses fed. Then
we'll see if old Skilly has got any vittles fit to put in a
hungry man's stomach."

Between them they carried the big grain box in from
the wagon and portioned out six generous measures of
oats. As they walked back past the long row of stalls,
Dan noticed one horse that still wore a saddle. It was a
big black one, with streaks of mud on its slender legs
and powerful haunches.

The boy hung back a step, staring into the stall. It
was hard to be certain in that light, but he thought he
recognized the animal. He wondered if he would find
the blue-cloaked rider inside the tavern.

They entered the back way, through the kitchen,
where a fine fragrance of roasting meat greeted their
noses. A big, angular woman stood by the fire with a
basting-spoon in her hand, and poured juices from the
drip pan over a brown leg of mutton. She eyed the pair
sharply and gave Silas Penny a curt nod. Then they
passed on into the "keeping-room."

There was a whale-oil lamp in one corner, over the bar, but its rays reached only a short distance into the steamy shadows of the big room. Such light as there was came mostly from the fire-place. It was nearly as high as Dan's head, and wide enough to take a six-foot log. On the long crane hung half a dozen pots of assorted sizes—kettles filled with toddy and mulled cider to warm a rain-soaked traveler's bones.

At least a score of men were sitting on the benches that flanked the hearth and standing in the red glow of the fire. Some were wagon-freighters like Silas Penny. One or two were drovers, convoying sheep and beef cattle to the city markets. And there was a scattering of local farmers, dropped in for the news and a mug of ale.

Dan looked in vain for the face of the man who had given him the dollar. He must have supped already and gone to a private room upstairs. Penny shouldered toward the bar. "A couple o' hot ciders, Skilly," he ordered jovially. "And lace mine with a bit o' rum. Stage is late, ain't it?"

"Aye," grumbled the sour-faced landlord. "Allus late when we're crowded. Keeps everybody waitin' to eat. Here's yer drinks."

The teamster tossed a coin on the bar and handed Dan a huge mug of spiced cider. The boy drank eagerly, the warm drink tingling pleasantly inside him. As he finished it there came the wailing note of a horn outside, and a general movement of the tipplers toward doors and windows.

"Stage is in!" bawled Skilly Bassett.

Dan could see a lantern moving outside, and hear the impatient jingle of harness as the hostler unhitched the lathered team. Then the door swung open to admit a huddle of chilly passengers from the coach. The men stamped and held out their hands to the blaze, calling loudly for drinks and supper. The two lady travelers retired in haste to the inn parlor where they could dry their wraps by the Franklin stove.

After a few minutes the tall woman from the kitchen —Dan decided she must be Mrs. Bassett—opened the door to shout that supper was ready. The coach passengers went into the dining-room first, followed immediately by the teamsters and drovers. Dan stuck close to Penny's side and took a place near the foot of the long deal table. There was no cloth upon it, but the food was plentiful and smelled delicious.

When everyone was seated, the innkeeper rose at the head of the table. "There bein' no minister present, I will say a brief grace," he announced in a nasal twang. And he went on to intone a blessing that might have been brief but seemed all too lengthy to the famished boy.

At last the smoking platters of mutton were set in motion. Then the boiled potatoes—the hubbard squash —the pickles and bread and butter. There was some polite conversation among the city folks at the other end of the table, but the teamsters were attending strictly to business. Dan also ate steadily, filling the deep hollow under his belt. Two kinds of pie—apple and mince—home-made cheese, hot tea and more mugs of cider completed the meal.

Silas Penny turned toward the boy at last with a twinkle in his eye. "Feelin' better?" he asked. "I'll say this fer Skilly. He may be 'tarnal mean most ways, but he sure sets a good table."

He looked at Dan thoughtfully. "Ye know," he said at length, "it mightn't be a bad idea fer you to stay on here a spell, workin' fer yer keep. Put some meat on yer bones. I reckon ye ain't in no special hurry to git on west, are ye? I could sort o' keep an eye on ye here, on my trips through. Maybe Bassetts don't need a boy but if ye want I can ask 'em in the mornin'."

Dan considered. "I'd like to get a place to stay for the winter," he said. "And I guess I could be some help around the stable. I get on fine with horses."

The big teamster clapped him on the shoulder. "All right, lad," he grinned, "I'll see what the ol' buzzard has to say."

They got up from the table and strolled back to the fire in the keeping-room. One by one the local patrons paid their scores and departed. The stage passengers were shown to chambers in the upper part of the house, and the teamsters began to choose their bed places on the sanded floor around the fire. At nine-thirty by the tall clock in the corner, Skilly Bassett pulled down the wooden wicket that hung over the bar and blew out the lamp.

"Good-night," he growled to the room at large, and shuffled off to bed.

Penny yawned and stretched his arms, then went to the window and looked out. "Wind's goin' down," he reported. "Rain's stopped an' there's a few stars out. Be cold an' clear tomorrer, I reckon."

He wrapped himself in his coat and lay down, feet to the fire. Dan followed his example. For a few minutes he stayed awake, enjoying the warmth and comparative comfort of his sleeping-place. Along the road he had slept in haystacks and under hedges. There would be no morning frost to stiffen his joints in this snug place.

There was no noise but the slow ticking of the clock, the crackle of the dying embers on the hearth, and the heavy breathing of the sleeping men around him. Soon his senses drowsed and he too fell into a deep slumber.

How long it lasted, Dan could not have told, nor did

he know what waked him. He raised himself quietly on one elbow and listened. Overhead somewhere a board creaked with a stealthy sound. Then he heard feet moving very softly on the stairs. One slow step at a time they drew nearer. The boy lay back on his side pretending sleep. But his eyes, accustomed now to the dark, could see the door-latch lifting. Inch by inch, the black line at the edge of the door widened. A tall, cloaked figure moved out of the shadow and silently entered the room.

TWO

DAN scarcely breathed as the man in the cloak tiptoed along the floor close to the wall. He passed a window and for a second his shape was outlined against the lighter darkness of the sky. The slim, devil-may-care grace of the figure—the jaunty angle of the bell-crowned hat—there was no mistaking him now. Dan knew he was again meeting his acquaintance of the road. But what was the fellow up to?

He had reached the corner of the room where the bar stood. Straining his ears, the boy thought he heard a faint grating of metal as if a key were being tried softly in a padlock. At that moment, a chunk of half-burned wood tumbled from the andirons with a thud that shattered the silence, and a flare of sparks made a sudden light in the room. Startled, Dan sat erect. He saw the man's arm make a quick movement, and before he knew it he was looking straight into the barrel of a pistol.

There was a long, breathless instant while they stared

at each other. Then the figure in the cloak moved quietly back along the wall toward the outside door. Still covering Dan with the pistol, he fumbled for the bolt, slid it back without a sound and pulled up the

latch. In a twinkling he was gone, closing the door behind him.

The boy heard the thud of his running feet on the ground outside and turned hastily to rouse the slumbering Penny. A shake or two woke the teamster and he sat up yawning. "What's all this?" he grumbled. "Surely 'tain't five yit!"

"No! No!" whispered Dan excitedly. "There was a man in here—one o' the guests—tryin' to rob the till! He saw me an' went out—to get his horse, I think!"

Penny was wide awake at last. He sprang up with a jump that shook the pine flooring. "Hey—Skilly Bassett!" he roared. "Rouse out, you snorin' lummoxes!" And he began kicking the men nearest him.

In the confusion that followed, it was Dan who had presence of mind to open the door and run into the yard. "Come on! He's out here—at the stable!" he called, but precious seconds were lost before the bewildered men began streaming out of the tavern. A light appeared upstairs and the landlord, in woolen nightgown and striped night-cap, thrust his head out the window. In his hands a blunderbuss waved to and fro threateningly.

"What's goin' on?" he screamed.

Before anyone had time to answer him there was a rattle of hooves on the gravel and a big horse flashed past the inn-door like a black thunderbolt. Leaning low on his neck was the man in the cloak and the bell-crowned hat.

The group stood speechless and watched him disappear in the dark. For a few seconds they could hear the swift tattoo of iron shoes on the road. There was a brief rumble as he crossed the bridge at the foot of the hill, then silence.

"Dad-blast his hide!" growled Silas Penny. "Gone! An' there ain't a nag in the township good enough to ketch him!"

The inn-keeper had lighted the lamp over the bar when they went inside once more, and one of the drovers had thrown a fresh log on the fire.

"Long's we're all waked up, how 'bout a round o' drinks, Skilly?" somebody suggested. "On the house, o' course!"

"Don't talk foolish!" squawked the landlord plaintively. "Ain't it enough that I've just been robbed?"

"Go on!" Silas Penny laughed. "Look in the till—you ain't lost a shillin', I'll warrant." He pushed Dan forward to the bar rail. "But you would have"—he continued triumphantly—"if it hadn't been fer this boy here!"

Drinks were poured, and while the audience gaped open-mouthed, the freighter told the story. On the bare facts Dan had given him he embroidered to such effect that in two minutes the youngster had become a hero. According to Penny's account Dan had even grappled with the robber, at imminent risk of his life.

"He'd ha' downed him, too, if the feller hadn't drawed a pistol!" the big teamster concluded. "Let's have a little more cider, Skilly. My throat's dry from talkin'."

"Did he look like a highwayman?" the stage-coach driver inquired. "What name did he give ye, Skilly?"

The landlord fished out a dog's-eared register from under the bar. "Here 'tis," he announced. " 'Mr. Lamb, of Boston.' Writ with quite a flourish, too. 'Mr. Lamb,' indeed! Mr. Wolf would ha' been closer to it! Lemme see—no, I wouldn't say he had the appearance of a scoundrel. Fair handsome, he was, an' dressed like a gentleman. Ordered the best brandy an' paid fer it in silver."

The tall clock struck two before they had thrashed the matter out and gone back to bed.

"Ho, hum!" yawned Penny as he stretched himself at Dan's side. "I hate to lose a whole hour o' sleep out o' the best part o' the night. But by thunder, I b'lieve ol' Bassett's bound to take ye on, now!"

.   .   .

The next time Dan woke there was pale morning light at the windows and the big tavern room was bustling with preparations for departure. The teamsters and drovers rubbed the sleep out of their eyes and went out to the pump in the yard to wash.

Energetic noises came from all over the premises. In the kitchen a serving-maid giggled loudly and clattered among the pans. A constant bleating of sheep and cackling of hens came from the pens behind the stable. Horses neighed and pawed the floor of their stalls. Stagecoach passengers dressed hastily in the rooms overhead, with a rattling of water pitchers and a clumping of boots. It was five o'clock.

As soon as Dan had washed he returned to the keeping-room to find his friend Silas Penny in earnest conversation with the landlord. From time to time one of them would glance in his direction, where he stood warming his hands before the fire. At length the freighter called to him.

"Danny," he said, "Mr. Bassett figgers maybe he could use a likely youngster 'round the place. Let's see— you're sixteen, ain't ye?"

Dan started to tell him he was a year younger, but Penny's hearty voice cut him off in haste. "Sixteen an' strong fer his age," he told the inn-keeper. "Powerful good with hosses, too. He'll earn five dollars a month an' keep, without a mite o' trouble."

At the mention of money Bassett's expression changed instantly. His mouth drew down sourly at the corners and he began to shake his head.

"Hold on, now, Skilly!" chuckled the big wagoner. "Don't let it upset ye so. Didn't he save ye five times that, last night? An' I tell ye he'll be worth every cent of it. Why, I'd trust this boy to handle my own team!

A man can't say more'n that."

"How do I know he ain't a runaway, like the last boy I had?" asked the landlord.

"I'll vouch fer him myself," Penny replied seriously. "I'll give my word ye won't regret takin' him."

"Wal—all right," said Bassett as if the words pained him. "But times is hard. I can't pay more'n four dollars—"

"It's a trade, then," answered the teamster briskly. "I'll see ye on the down-trip, Danny. Now where in tunket is my breakfast?"

"Table's set an' ready," Bassett told him. "Go git it. No, not you, boy—you'll eat later when the early chores is done. Skip out an' tell Tim Garrity at the stable that I've hired ye. Help him hitch up the rigs, an' anything else he wants ye to do."

"Thank you, Mr. Bassett!" Dan said earnestly. "I'll try to give satisfaction." And with that he was out the door at a run.

He found the Irishman inside the barn, whistling and swearing by turns as he fed and watered the horses.

"Begob, an' it's a wonder the ould skinflint'd iver think I needed help!" he exclaimed when Dan told him the news. "More power t'ye, lad! There's the curry-comb in the rack, an' the coach-horses could do wid a bit o' groomin'. Mind that off leader's heels. He's touchy but he don't mean no harm."

Dan went to work eagerly. He had a knack of making horses feel at home with him, and even the touchy off leader was soon munching away at his grain while the boy curried his muddy flanks. There was no time for thorough grooming—"just a lick an' a promise," Garrity told him. But in ten minutes he had all four of the stage-horses looking reasonably ready for the road.

"So ye're the b'y as chased out the robber last night!" the Irishman remarked. "A bad 'un—that feller. But what a horse! As pretty a trav'ler as iver I laid me eyes on! I was slapin' in the loft over the shed, an' whin I heard the racket I was downstairs like a shot. By then, though, he had the barn-door open an' out he come, a-tearin'."

A deep, jolly voice interrupted the hostler at this point. "What—talkin' again an' delayin' the United States mails?" it boomed, and Dan turned to see the stage-driver standing behind them, whip in hand. He was a stout, red-faced man in boots, a homespun greatcoat and battered slouch hat. Dan had heard his name in the tavern the night before. He was Nate Gilman—a famous personage up and down the pike. It was his boast that in twenty years of driving over those New Hampshire hills he had never lost a wheel or upset a coach.

"Ready, are ye, Natey?" Tim Garrity replied. "Well, so are we. Come, lad, lend a hand wid the harness."

They slipped on the collars, buckled the hames and led the two teams out to the coach. A flock of sheep and a dozen fat cattle filled the yard as the drovers began their day's journey. Their shouts and the constant barking of their herd-dogs made the place a bedlam.

"Hi!" yelled Garrity. "Git them bastes out o' the way. Can't ye see the stage is ready?"

Gradually the animals streamed into the high road and were headed east up the hill. And no sooner was the yard cleared than Nate Gilman, on the box, picked up a long, curved cow-horn and blew a melodious blast. There was a scraping of chairs in the dining-room. A moment later the passengers came hurrying forth. Their leather trunks and band-boxes were strapped securely in the great boot at the back of the coach, the ladies were helped in by the gentlemen, the driver unfurled the twelve-foot lash of his whip and cracked it artistically over the backs of his team, Tim Garrity sprang away from the leaders' tossing heads—and with a roar and a rattle the stage went out of the yard.

"Have to step lively, lad!" the hostler called, as Dan stood staring after the departing coach. "Them teamsters'll be next."

Together they began putting harness on the six-horse

teams of the freight wagons. Dan led out Silas Penny's big roan wheelers and dropped the wagon tongue between them. As he hooked the traces he saw his friend approaching across the yard.

Penny grinned. "Durned if ye don't act like ye b'longed in the job," he greeted him. "Old wagon looks pretty good, in daylight, don't she?" He cast an eye

over the snowy canvas top and the boat-shaped, red-painted sides of the huge vehicle.

Dan agreed with him. "That's a Pennsylvania wagon, isn't it?" he asked.

"Yessir—built in Lancaster," the freighter told him. "Don't see many like that 'round here. When the British had the harbors blockaded, durin' the war, it was these 'stogy wagons that hauled most o' the goods 'tween Pennsylvania an' New England. Nothin' like 'em ever built fer pullin' on a good road. Ton-to-a-hoss is what I haul, an' I can make my twenty mile a day 'thout gallin' 'em or ga'ntin' 'em."

They brought out the swing-team and the leaders,

and hitched them up. The three other wagons in the yard were also ready. Their drivers stood in a little group cracking jokes and roaring with laughter as they filled and lit their pipes.

"Wal, Danny," said the burly wagoner, "it's past six o'clock. Sun'll be a-poppin' over the hill 'fore long. Time I was hittin' the road. Guess I don't have to give ye no good advice. Ol' Skilly's mean an' he'll work ye hard, but he keeps his word. I'll be haulin' through to Boston again in a week or so, an' I'll be lookin' fer ye."

He gathered the six reins in his huge left fist and pursed his lips in a whistle. At the shrill sound the roans pricked up their ears, gathered their feet and leaned into their collars like one horse. The stout leather creaked, the bells tinkled, and the wheels began to roll.

Dan felt pretty lonesome when the last of the four big wagons had swung out on the pike. He watched them start up the hill, the black pots of axle-grease swinging rhythmically between the rear wheels. Silas Penny waved an arm to him and he waved back. Then he saw Tim Garrity at his side.

"What wud a b'y like you be doin' gawkin' after wagons, an' it past breakfast time?" he asked kindly. "Come wid me, now, an' let's see if they've saved a bit for the stable hands."

"I've been a heap hungrier than this," Dan told him.

"That supper last night was the first real meal I'd sat down to in four days. I ate enough to last me a while. Still—I guess I could manage somethin' now."

They went to the pump and washed their hands, then to the kitchen door. A clatter of dishes came from inside. Two red-cheeked country girls, who helped Mrs. Bassett with the housework, caught a fit of the giggles as Dan entered with the hostler. The good lady herself looked up sharply from the pie-board where she was rolling dough and gave a disparaging sniff.

"Late again," she snapped. "Set down an' eat so's we can git on with our work. Sue—fetch the mush."

A bowl of Indian meal porridge was set in front of Dan, together with a squat, blue pitcher of molasses. He poured some of the thick, dark stuff over his mush, picked up his spoon and fell to work.

"Don't mind the ould 'un," whispered Garrity. "Sour as a choke-cherry, but she's a rare cook."

Indeed Dan found even such simple fare as the mush seemed to taste better than any he had eaten before. And the crude, tangy sweetness of the black-strap molasses flavored it to perfection. When it was finished he pushed back the bowl and started to rise, thinking his breakfast was over. But now the serving-girl appeared with plates of pork sausage and fried potatoes, and mugs of golden cider. Under the table edge, the boy let out his belt a notch. Then he went on with the meal. At last, full almost to bursting, he left his empty plate to follow Tim into the yard.

"Golly!" he sighed with content. "This time yesterday I sure never thought I'd be feelin' like this today."

THREE

DAN had a few moments of leisure before returning to the stable chores. He had been asleep in the back of the 'stogy wagon when he arrived at the inn the night before. And since then he had been too much occupied to get a real view of his new surroundings. Now he walked out to the road and looked about him.

The "Fox and Stars" was a big, square-built frame building of two and a half stories, set with its gable end to the turnpike. Between the house and the edge of the road fifty feet of grassy lawn intervened, and in this space grew a pair of gigantic elms, lofty and umbrella-shaped, spreading their shade over the tavern and a fair part of the yard. The sign-board swung from the cross arm of a tall oak post, close to the road. Its colors had been somewhat faded by the weather but the crude painting of a bright red fox, against a background of dark blue with three white stars, was still clearly discernible.

Above the picture was lettering which read: "Entertainment for Man and Beast," and beneath it, filling the bottom of the board, the name "S. BASSETT."

The tavern had been built on a level stretch of road between the ascent to the eastward hilltop and the drop

to the river on the west. Below him, half a mile away, Dan could see a bridge and the roofs of a village among trees. The spire of a church stood sharp and white against the green of pines and the gold and russet of hardwoods on the opposite hill.

Up and down the valley of the narrow, winding little river, the boy saw farms spread out—stone-walled fields and pastures—apple orchards—white-painted houses and weathered gray barns.

It was a good, thrifty country, settled for close to a hundred years and made fruitful by generations of solid farmers.

Turning back to the tavern he looked over the rest of the buildings. An "L," two stories in height, extended from the rear end of the main structure, and was joined to the barn by a series of low sheds, used for storing firewood, old sleighs and carriages and spare sets of harness. Then came the big stable, offset from the line of sheds so that its great front door opened directly on the inn-yard. It had stalls for forty horses and a capacious hay-loft overhead. Still further back were a chicken-house, hog-house, and fenced enclosures with open sheds where the drovers penned up their flocks for the night.

Mowing-fields and stony pasture-land ran back up the hill to the edge of the woods. The air was still sharp with autumn chill but it was a fine morning. Dan began to feel at home in this place.

As the day advanced he found there was plenty of work to do. However, to a boy as fond of horses as he was, it was pleasant work. He helped Tim Garrity clean out the stalls and put fresh straw in the empty ones. Then the relay-horses for the down coach had to be curried and brushed. Next he was initiated into the mysteries of cleaning harness. It was well along in the morning when Tim slapped his thigh suddenly and swore.

"That bay mare o' Skilly's!" he ejaculated. "Begob, I clean forgot! She cast a shoe yesterday an' wan of us'll have to take her to the smithy. Think ye cud do it, lad? Just a step it is—down the hill, this side o' the bridge. Tell Ben Tucker to remember the shoe needs weightin' a bit forrard an' on the inside. Hop spry an' ye'll be back 'fore dinner."

Dan found the mare in a roomy box-stall at the end of the line. Her name—"Lady"—was painted in fancy letters on the top plank of the gate. The boy slipped a halter over her head and led her out. As her glossy bay flanks caught the light from the wide barn-door he had to stop and stare in sheer admiration. It was the first clear view he had had of the inn-keeper's favorite driving horse.

"Golly!" he breathed. "You're a lady, all right. Whoever named you was sensible!"

She stood about fifteen hands, fine in the legs and clean in the barrel. Her deep chest and smooth-muscled quarters told of trotting speed and endurance. And her head was lovely to behold.

The mare investigated Dan's jacket sleeve with a velvety black nose, and widened her nostrils in a coquettish little snort.

"Ye'll find her gentle as a kitten," said Garrity. "But take good care of her, for she's the apple o' the ould man's eye!"

Dan led her out of the yard and down the hill. The blacksmith shop was not hard to find. From a distance he could hear the musical ring of the anvil under the smith's hammer. There were a couple of work-horses tied under the trees, and a boy about Dan's own age was sitting on a farm-wagon with one wheel missing, swinging his heels. A wide grin split his freckled face.

"You're the new boy at the tavern, ain't you?" he said. "My name's Ethan Hayes. What's yours?"

"Dan Drew. Your wagon broke down?"

"Jest gittin' a new tire put on. Ben'll be through pretty quick an' you can have Lady shod. Beauty, ain't she?"

"Pretty as a picture," Dan replied. "I bet she can step, too."

"Took Skilly's gig to Marlboro once in an hour 'n' a quarter. That's two stages—close on twenty mile."

Dan whistled. "I reckoned she was fast, but that's great roadin'," he said, impressed.

There came a great hissing from the doorway of the smithy, as Ben Tucker plunged the wheel, with its red-hot tire, into a half-hogshead of water.

"Here y' are, sonny," he called. "Good fer another ten year, tell yer paw."

Dan turned the mare's halter over to the smith and

gave his new acquaintance a hand with the heavy wheel. A swab of tallow was smeared on the axle and the hub slipped on, to be secured with a wedge-shaped iron pin.

"Look," said the freckle-faced lad. "That white barn on the hill is our place. Come on up when ye git a spell off. I got a dog that's sure death on woodchucks. We can have some fun."

He hitched up his team and drove off with a wave to the tavern boy. Dan looked after him a trifle wistfully. He couldn't help envying a boy who had a real home and a family.

"Wal, youngster," said the blacksmith jovially, "I see they trusted ye with the bay mare. That means they think right well of ye, up to the Fox an' Stars. She's lost her off front shoe, ain't she? An' I'll wager that Irishman told ye to remind me about weightin' it forrard an' inside! As if I didn't know her like a sister!"

He roared with good-natured laughter as his great, hairy arm pumped the leather bellows and the forge fire spurted into flame. Ben Tucker was all that a smith should be—a big, black, bearded man with a voice like the rumbling bass of a church organ. He chose a light blank shoe and shaped it swiftly and with amazing deftness.

"So-o, girl, so-o," he said gently, as he picked up the mare's forefoot and held it on his leather-aproned knee.

The shoe was almost a perfect fit. He gave it a few final touches and set it aside while he trimmed the dainty hoof with his big two-handled knife. Then with quick strokes he nailed on the shoe. The mare put her foot on

the floor, tested it with a stamp or two and rested her weight on it comfortably.

"Like it, do ye?" asked the smith, giving her gleaming neck a pat. "Let's see the rest o' yer feet."

One by one he examined the other three shoes, tapping a nail tight here and there. "Now she'll do," he told the boy. "Fit to step a two-forty mile right this minute."

As Dan led the graceful trotter back toward the tavern, a chaise rattled past him up the hill. It was drawn by a big-boned, hammer-headed brown horse—a puller with the bit clamped firmly between his foaming jaws. Slouched under the leather hood of the two-wheeled carriage was a short, hugely fat man with a reddish circle of chin whiskers. They went tearing up the grade, the horse's big hooves flinging out stones at every stride, and turned into the inn-yard a short distance ahead of the boy. When he got there the fat man was climbing with some difficulty over the wheel and Tim Garrity was holding the horse's tossing head.

Skilly Bassett came hurriedly out of the keeping-room, wiping his hands on his white apron.

"Howdy-do, Asa—howdy-do," he greeted the new-comer. "Fine mornin' fer this late in the fall. S'pose ye're here 'bout that 'tempted robbery we had las' night. Well, come right in an' wet yer whistle. You, Danny—soon's ye've put the mare in her stall, come to the house. Reckon the constable may want to ask ye some questions."

Tim Garrity led the brown horse to the barn and called to Dan, who was stabling the mare. "Did iver ye see such a solid-built feller? That's Asa Pease—the town constable. Mind what ye tell him. He's sharper'n ye'd think from the look of him."

Dan went to the tavern door and was beckoned inside by the inn-keeper. One or two loungers were drinking mugs of cider in a corner. On the big bench beside the fire the constable sat, his huge belly resting on his knees. His little, half-closed eyes regarded Dan across a foaming pint-pot of ale.

"Boy," he said suddenly in a high, sing-song voice,

"boy—what did this robber look like?"

Dan swallowed nervously. "He was tall—six feet or a little over, I should think, but Mr. Bassett could tell you that." He considered a moment. "You see he passed me on the road yesterday and I got a close look at his face. A handsome sort of man, very pale, with black hair. His hat was off and I could see black locks comin' down over his forehead. His eyes were very light gray and so sharp it was like they bored right through you."

"Wait!" interrupted Mr. Pease. "Ye say the hair came down over his forehead. Didn't see the wind blow it back, by chance?"

"No," Dan answered, mystified.

The constable turned to Bassett. "That don't git us much further," he snapped. "I thought the lad might've seen a brand. There's one or two scoundrels loose, 'twixt here an' Boston that has H.T. burned on their foreheads—meanin' hoss-thief. By the way, Skilly—that hoss o' his—ever seen him before?"

The tavern-keeper shook his head. "Finest nag we've had in the stable in years, but strange to me. Must have stood sixteen an' a half hands—coal black. Ain't many hosses like that 'round these parts."

From outside came the pealing note of a horn.

"Stage!" exclaimed Bassett. "Dan, hop out there an' help Tim with the change o' teams."

The Boston-bound coach mounted the hill and pulled into the tavern yard at a trot.

"Catch the leaders' heads, lad, while I unhook," Garrity called. He worked quickly, loosing the wheel team from the double-trees, then moving up behind the leaders and freeing their traces. "Right-o! Take 'em

away!" he ordered and Dan trotted stableward with a hand on each bridle.

Right behind him Garrity followed with the wheelers. The four horses entered their regular stalls and stood without hitching while the fresh team, already harnessed, was led out. Several passengers had left the coach to stretch their legs or get a drink in the bar. With both Tim and Dan fastening the traces and hold-back straps the new relay was ready in a matter of three or four minutes, and a blast of the horn brought a scurry of travelers to regain their places.

"Smartly done, lad!" shouted the coachman. "They

don't change hosses faster in Boston!" He released the brake, cracked his long whip, and the fresh four jumped eagerly into their collars.

Dan watched the big conveyance roll out of the yard and drew a long breath of admiration. It was a new coach, built in Concord. Square on top and curved underneath, it differed both from the old four-bench wagon stages of a generation earlier, and from the light, egg-shaped Trenton coaches then in use on many of the roads. It was sturdy, roomy and comfortable, and had a railed space for luggage on top as well as in the "boot" behind. It held eight inside passengers and two more could be accommodated on the roof behind the driver. The body was slung on stout leather thorough-braces that cushioned it from the jolting of the wheels. With its black and yellow paint glistening in the sun, the coach was as eye-filling a sight as one could wish to see.

Back in the stable, Dan helped the hostler rub down the sweating team that had just been unharnessed. They were splendid horses, bred for coach work and perfectly matched in color. All four were chestnuts, the leaders a trifle on the small side but compact and fiery, with the clean-limbed endurance of the Morgan breed. The wheelers were bigger-boned and somewhat heavier— good pullers. They would weigh, Dan judged, about twelve hundred pounds apiece.

As he hung up the curry-comb he saw the fat constable waddling toward the barn. "Boy!" came his squeaky, nasal call. "Boy, fetch my rig."

The brown horse, still in the shafts, had been fastened inside the stable. Dan hastily untied his hitch-rope and led him out.

"He'll stand," said Asa Pease. "I'll need your hand to git over the wheel." He heaved one foot up to the hub, and resting part of his weight on Dan's shoulder, succeeded in swinging his bulk into the sagging chaise.

"Look ye, now," he said, turning his sharp little eyes on the boy's face. "Think ye'd recognize that robber if ever ye should see him?"

Dan nodded. "I'm sure I would."

" 'Cause some night," the constable finished, "unless I'm mighty mistook, he's liable to be ridin' again."

FOUR

DAN was tired by the time darkness fell, ending his first day as stable-boy at the Fox and Stars. Supper time came, and with it the arrival of the usual freight-wagon men, a drover with a belated flock of sheep, a private carriage or two—and last but not least, the coach. Skilly Bassett came into the kitchen while the boy was eating his bread and milk. With a full tavern he was in a good humor. "Ye done all right today," he said, rubbing his hands. "Soon's ye git the hang o' things, ye might even be worth yer keep. Tim'll give ye a blanket an' ye kin bed in the barn. But mind—no smokin' or such foolishness!"

He returned to the keeping-room and Dan took his lonesome way out to the stable. There was a heap of loose hay in one corner of the dark floor. He took the clean old horse-blanket the hostler had given him and wrapped himself in it. The hay rustled and settled under him, giving comfort to his work-weary muscles. He had slept in far worse beds than this, and he had the horses to keep him company. Their big bodies warmed the barn and their pungent smell mingled pleasantly with the fragrance of hay. From time to time they moved gently, shifting their weight, sighing, nuzzling in the corners of their cribs for lost wisps of fodder. There was a faint chirping of crickets from deep in the mows. The stable cat passed by, intent on her night's hunting. Many little sounds made up a soft, breathing monotone that was more restful than stillness.

Dan lay awhile, staring into the dark. He was at the beginning of a new life, but he could not leave the old one without a backward glance.

Very dimly he could remember the big, bluff sailor-man who was his father. He could remember the excitement in the house when Ebenezer Drew came home from a voyage and roaring with laughter, scooped up the toddler to set him on his shoulder. Dan was three then. And from the next sailing his father never returned.

For two years after that, Patience Drew had kept the neat cottage with the wild roses in the door-yard, and fed herself and her small son by taking in sewing. Then a long illness had come. Without relatives who could help them, the pair had been forced to move out of their home. A wealthy but crotchety old Portsmouth spinster gave them shelter in return for Mrs. Drew's services as a maid-of-all-work, and it was in her house that Dan had grown up. Most of his out-of-school hours were spent at the various neighbors', where he did stable-chores for such odd pennies as he could pick up. He had no inclination toward the sea. While his school-mates were sailing skiffs and setting lobster-pots, he was grooming horses and learning to handle the reins.

Dan's mother had never fully recovered from her earlier illness, and the hard work she did had gradually worn her down. He remembered the day in late August when he had come in and found her sitting on her bed, her face in her wasted hands. "Danny," she told him then, "it's no use keeping it from you—I won't be here much longer." He had stopped the slow flowing of her tears and tried clumsily to reassure her, but her words were true. In September they had laid her to rest in the little grass-grown burying-ground that looked toward the blue water.

Perhaps because the desolate loneliness of that moment haunted him, Dan had wished to turn his back on the sea forever. From the freight-teamsters who hauled their produce to the busy docks of Portsmouth he had heard stories of the fine back-country farms and the still more marvelous country opening up to the west. It was in that direction he decided to go. And now—well, here he was. He pillowed his head on his arm and closed his eyes, wondering as he fell asleep how long it would be before he felt the urge to wander on again.

•   •   •

The boy woke to the gusty beat of rain on the roof, and for two days an autumn storm held the valley in its grip. Drenched wagoners beat their arms in the inn-yard and downed great mugs of hot flip in the taproom. The coach-horses came in, mud-splattered and steaming at the end of each stage. The last brown leaves were stripped from the trees and heaped in sodden windrows along the fences.

Dan worked, indoors and out, and when the wet and cold became unbearable he could always accompany Tim Garrity to the kitchen, and crouch by the roaring cook-fire. Mrs. Bassett—"Black Maria" as the Irishman was wont to call her—eyed the pair with a cold disfavor. She had her own rigid standards of housekeeping and considered mud, tracked into her kitchen by stable boots, to be an abomination.

"Sue," she would say acidly, "fetch that mop an' see if ye kin git the floor lookin' like somethin' besides a pig-pen."

When the rain ceased, a period of fine, frosty autumn weather came on. The corn was all husked and in the cribs; the pumpkins gathered; the houses banked with brush and earth against the coming of winter.

43

One of Dan's chores was to carry in wood for the four mighty fire-places that warmed the tavern and cooked the food. Sawed and split the previous winter, it was piled in great stacks in one of the sheds between house and barn. It took real muscle to handle an armful of those solid oak and maple chunks. At first the boy's back ached from the work. However, with plenty of wholesome food and sleep his thin body quickly built itself up, and within a few weeks he was carrying the loads with ease.

The lusty life of the turnpike went on as always. The big freight wagons toiled over the road at a quickened pace, their drivers anxious to get as much tonnage as possible to the coast before snow flew. Whenever Silas Penny hauled through, he stopped for a chat with Dan. On his first trip from Bellows Falls he brought the boy a thick, warm jacket of blue homespun.

The boy's eyes shone as he tried it on. "Gee, Mr. Penny," he stammered, "you were mighty good to think o' this. I'll pay for it soon as I get some wages."

" 'Deed ye won't!" snorted the teamster. "That there's a gift from my missus. Wove on her own loom out o' real Green Mountain wool. We lost our only youngster when he wa'n't much higher'n my knee. Guess that's why she likes to do things fer boys that need 'em."

AN AUTUMN STORM HELD THE VALLEY
IN ITS GRIP

He turned away and blew his nose violently into the red bandanna handkerchief he carried in the pocket of his butternut breeches.

It was in the fourth week of Dan's stay at the tavern that preparations began to be made for the annual "harvest-hum." Never having attended one of these celebrations he was somewhat mystified at first, but Tim soon enlightened him.

"Wait till ye see the mountains o' food an' the rivers o' drink they set out!" said the Irishman, smacking his lips. "All the folks both up the road an' down will be on hand fer the shenanigan. The fiddlers'll be playin' an' the lads an' colleens dancin' till the cocks start to crow in the mornin'."

For two days before the event Mrs. Bassett was baking bread and pies and cakes and frying doughnuts. Many of the Deptford housewives would bring their own delicacies to the feast, but others would buy the supper prepared at the inn. Tim Garrity was called upon to help the tavern-keeper roll barrels of cider, ale and Medford rum up from the cellar. Dan was sent on numerous errands to the village, to requisition spare plates and cups and bone-handled steel knives and two-tined forks.

By sundown on the day of the harvest-home, a dozen chaises, wagons and carriages were hitched along the

inn-yard fence, and more were rolling up the hill each
moment. A few young blades rode their saddle-horses,
and Uncle Mose Morrison, from Half Moon Pond,
brought his plump wife on a wooden pillion, rigged behind him on the broad back of his work mare.

For this occasion all the ground-floor rooms of the
tavern had been thrown open. Not only the big keeping-room but the parlor, across the center hall, and the
dining-room were filled with a chattering crowd. Long
board-and-trestle tables were set up, and chairs, stools
and benches stood in ranks on either side.

At six o'clock the steaming food was on the tables
and Ben Tucker's deep voice roared out an invitation to
all to take their places. Even Dan had been invited in
from the barn. With his face carefully scrubbed, his one
suit brushed and his unruly brown hair slicked down
with water, he stood behind his stool at the foot of one
of the tables while the minister of Deptford Congrega-
tional Church invoked a blessing. Then what a scraping
of chairs and clatter of tableware followed! The boards
were literally bending under the weight of good things
to eat and there was no delay in falling to work.

There were huge, deep chicken pies, whole boiled
hams, platters of roast beef and legs of mutton; potatoes
both boiled and fried, hubbard squash and stewed
onions; vast mounds of hot biscuits and snowy bread,

bowls of gravy, dishes of preserves and pickles, pats of
fresh-churned butter; brown-crusted pies of tart fall
apples, golden pumpkin pies, rich, suety mince pies
redolent of cider; cakes made and frosted according to
all the town's most famous recipes; white sugar cookies,
brown molasses cookies, hickory and black walnut cookies; doughnuts round and doughnuts twisted. There
were pitchers of coffee for the older folks, milk or sweet
cider for the youngsters. Occasionally a farmer would
wink at his neighbor and go to the bar for a taste of
something stronger, but it was a good-humored and
well-behaved gathering.

Dan looked about, when he had eaten all he could
hold, and noticed how many children had come to the
supper. There were scores of boys and girls of his own
age or younger, and even a few babes in arms. Up at the
farther end of the room he caught sight of the red head
of Ethan Hayes. The farm-boy was munching manfully
on a big twisted doughnut. His jaws worked slower and
slower, till at last he sighed regretfully and dropped the
remaining morsel on his plate.

The sound of a girl's laugh came to Dan, and across
the table from his freckle-faced acquaintance he caught
sight of a pair of snapping black eyes.

"That last one finished you, Ethan!" cried the girl.
"I've kept count. Four doughnuts—three cookies—a

piece of apple pie—and—"

"Hush, Molly!" commanded the red-cheeked woman beside her. "Mind your manners. Ethan knows it's the polite thing to do well by the vittles, an' it certainly is *not* polite to notice how much other folks eat!"

"All right, Mother," the miss replied demurely. "But he did look so sorrowful when he had to give up! Come on, Ethan, let's go in the parlor an' start some games. Let the old folks sit here an' gab, if they like."

She rose, beckoning to a dozen other boys and girls sitting at the two long tables. As Ethan Hayes got up to follow her his glance fell on Dan and he grinned. The stable-boy felt his cheeks flushing. He tried to busy himself with his empty plate and pretend he had not been noticed. Then Tim Garrity, whose seat was beside his own, laid a hand on his knee. "Don't be missin' the fun, lad," he whispered. "That Molly Crandall's the prettiest young 'un in the township, an' it was herself asked the redhead to invite ye!"

Bashfully Dan got to his feet and followed the crowd of young people into the inn parlor. There were three or four boys older and bigger than himself, a few who were smaller, and a number of girls of assorted ages. They looked at him curiously but without hostility. There were no introductions. Ethan simply said, "Come on, Dan—we're goin' to play games. What'll we start with,

Molly?"

Molly Crandall flashed a boyish smile in Dan's direction. She was tall and strong and brown, with thick, dark pigtails down her back. "Oh, Drop-the-Handkerchief's as good as any to begin with," she answered. "Make your ring an' I'll be It."

They joined hands and the fun got under way, to an accompaniment of shouts and squeals. A minute later Dan had forgotten himself in the game. He no longer felt awkward. He was enjoying himself. They went on to play "On the Green Carpet," and "Through the Needle's Eye," with the customary forfeits. One of the lisping older girls suggested "Postoffice," but Molly vetoed the idea.

"I don't mind kissing when it's a forfeit," she said, "but when the boys start putting twenty or thirty stamps on their letters you can count me out."

"Guess we can't play anyhow," Ethan put in. "I kin hear the fiddles startin' to scrape. They'll want this room fer a square dance."

There was shouting and laughter from the older people as they made up their sets of eight and took their places wherever they could make room. The boys and girls went to sit in out-of-the-way corners where they could watch without being in the way. The fiddles began to squeak a lively tune, feet tapped in time, and

Uncle Mose Morrison, the most famous "caller" between the Merrimack and the Connecticut, started the sing-song doggerel that announced the first figure.

"All hands 'round for birdie-in-the-cage;
    Swing to the left an' keep in step—
  Back to the right an' hold on tight—
    Allemande left an' a right-hand chain—
  Swing 'er when you meet 'er an' run away home—
    First couple out an' make yer bow—
  Second couple out an' four hands 'round—
    Birdie-in-the-cage an' the cage is thin—
  Birdie flies out an' crow flies in—"

Round and round whirled the homespun farmers and their buxom wives to the lilting scream of the fiddles. There was such a stamping and shouting that the solid timbers of the tavern shook. Dan's eyes shone and his boot-heels kept time to the rhythm of the dance.

Without knowing just how he got there, he had found himself sitting on the narrow stairs, with Molly Crandall wedged in beside him. There came a lull when the first figure ended, and he heard her voice.

"Why don't you come to school, Dan Drew?"

"Aw—" he replied shyly—"I ain't—I haven't got time. You see I work here for my keep."

"Humph," she replied. "You'd think Skilly could let

you off four or five hours in the middle o' the day. Plenty of boys do their chores before and after school."

Dan shook his head. "He don't think I'm worth what he's s'posed to pay me, even yet," he answered. "Besides, I went to school up till this year."

"Yes—but don't you want to be really educated—go to Dartmouth College maybe, and be a famous man like Mr. Daniel Webster?"

"I hadn't thought much about it," Dan told her.

"Listen!" she exclaimed, and laid a friendly hand on his shoulder. "I know what I'll do. Father's got loads of books—I could bring you some to read."

"I'd like that," said Dan. "I like to read all right. But I'm 'fraid it won't work. You see I sleep in the barn, an' I don't dast light a candle, 'mongst all that hay."

"Oh, dear," she frowned. "Then we'll have to wait till summer, when it stays light in the evenings. But we'll do it then!"

"Yes," said Dan. "That'll be mighty nice of you, an' I sure will take good care o' the books."

It was the first time he had thought of staying on permanently in Deptford. But this girl was taking it for granted that he was a fixture in the community. It gave him a pleasant feeling—as if he amounted to something after all.

Together they watched the dancing for another hour. Ben Tucker cutting pigeon-wings and roaring out the choruses of the songs. Pompous Squire Pierce with the great gold seals of his watch chain jouncing up and down on his round stomach. Even Maria Bassett laugh-

ing, as old Skilly whirled her in obedience to the caller's "Swing yer partners!"

With the arrival of the stage, Dan was called away to put up the horses, and soon after they were stabled he went to bed. But from his nest in the hay he could hear the merriment going forward till after midnight. He roused from his dozing to catch the sound of cheery good-nights and the creak of wheels in the yard, then fell into a deep sleep, as stillness settled over the valley. It was something less than an hour later that he was wakened again. This time it was to a sound of angry shouting and pounding on the tavern door.

He heard Skilly Bassett's sleepy voice squalling a question from the upstairs window, then a loud voice in reply.

"Rouse the village!" came the shout. "Don't ye know me, man? I'm Squire Pierce. I've been robbed!"

FIVE

DAN rubbed the sleep out of his eyes and sat up, trying to collect his thoughts. The squire—robbed! Pulling on his boots and jacket, he stumbled the dark length of the barn floor and opened the door a foot or two. There was no moon, but in the cold, bright starlight he could see the dark bulk of the squire's carriage and the two panting horses. Bassett was hurrying downstairs with a lantern. By the time the boy crossed the yard the tavern door was flung open and there stood the landlord in his flannel nightshirt and nightcap.

"My land, Squire!" Skilly shivered. "Ye give me a turn! Robbed, did ye say?"

"Aye!" stormed the plump justice. "At the pistol's point! Forty dollars, he took, and my gold watch and seals! We'd got only a little beyond the bridge when the fellow rode his horse up abreast and ordered me to stop! He can't have gone far though, for I drove directly back."

"Quick, Dan!" the inn-keeper cried. "Saddle the gray

an' spread the word. Best ride straight to Asa Pease's first. That's out the Jaffrey road, close to the town line. Big white house on the left. I'll send Tim fer the nearer folks. We ought to have a posse inside of an hour."

Dan ran back to the stable, his heart pounding with excitement. In the dark he couldn't find a saddle, but he had often ridden bareback. In thirty seconds he had the old gray horse out of his stall and slipped the bit of a work bridle into his mouth. Then he was clattering out of the yard. It was fortunate that the nag was sure-footed, for he galloped him recklessly down the hill. Out on the dark south road to Jaffrey the gray began to puff, but Dan urged him on with a heel in the ribs whenever he showed signs of slowing.

Past them flew trees and stone walls and slumbering, black-windowed farm-houses. Once the boy thought he heard the thud of another horse's hooves, but it must have been an echo, for when he pulled over to the road-side grass, the sound was gone. Two miles—three miles he rode, and the pale shape of a house loomed up on his left. Was that the place? He hated to wake the inmates if he was wrong. Without dismounting, he sat on his horse in the front yard and shouted at the top of his lungs.

"Hello! Hello the house!"

There was no answer for a moment. Just as he was

preparing to shout again one of the windows opened with a creaking sound.

"Who's yellin' at this hour o' the night?" came the peevish, piping voice of the constable.

"Dan Drew, from the tavern," the boy replied. "There's been a robbery. Squire Pierce, it was. Mr. Bassett sent me to fetch you."

The fat man appeared to consider these statements. Then he sighed. "Wait an' help me harness my hoss," he said, and slammed the window shut. In a surprisingly short time he came waddling out, fully dressed and carrying a tin lantern.

Dan lent him a hand with the gig and the big brown horse, then mounted again and rode beside him. At the rapid pace they went it was difficult to converse, but by the time they reached the inn he had managed to give the constable such details as he knew.

Quite a number of villagers had assembled in the meantime. There were all kinds of weapons in evidence, ranging from shot-guns and squirrel rifles to pitchforks and butcher-knives, and the yard was full of gigs and "shays," saddle-horses and barebacked work nags.

Asa Pease did not climb down. Instead the crowd swarmed around his wheels, their lanterns bobbing like fire-flies, and in his high, flat-toned voice he began to shoot questions and give orders. First of all, Squire Pierce was asked about the robber's appearance. A tallish man, he thought, in a dark cloak and beaver hat.

"Same one!" nodded Pease. "An' the hoss—big, black one—fine-lookin'?"

No, the squire had an impression of a rather small horse—bay or brown, with one white stocking.

"That's better!" snapped the constable. "Means we got some chance o' ketchin' him." Rapidly he assigned parties of three or four to follow each road out of the village. "If ye don't find nothin'," he concluded, "we'll meet back here 'round seven o'clock."

Dan had hoped he would be picked to accompany one of the posses, but Skilly put a stop to that. "Got to have somebody to guard the stables," he said. "Might be a slick plan to steal hosses. Here"—he put a huge old pistol in the boy's hand—"mind ye don't shoot it off an' hurt nothin'!"

Filled with the importance of his post, Dan closed the barn door all but a narrow crack, and perched himself just inside on a half-bushel measure, the heavy horsepistol across his knees. From this vantage point he could command a view of most of the yard and catch the sound of any approach. He sat there straining his eyes into the shadowy night, his nerves so tense that he could hear the pounding of his own pulse.

What if the highwayman *should* return—to make

away with the tavern horses while all the men were out hunting him? Dan gripped the stock of the pistol tight and hoped it was properly primed. But nothing hap-

pened. He heard a dog begin barking, miles away at the outer edge of the township. Other dogs, far and near, took up the chorus, then grew tired of it and the drowsy silence descended again. Once or twice he found his head nodding and straightened himself up with a jerk. Then before he knew it he was asleep—dreaming un-

easily of a white, reckless face and a black cloak and a
bell-crowned beaver hat.

It was some time later that his dreams were shattered
by a thunderous *bang!* Scared half out of his wits, the
boy sprang up, shaking, clinging to the edge of the
doorway. On the floor his pistol still smoked. It must
have fallen from his knees and discharged itself, missing
his feet by a miracle. Outside, the stars were beginning
to pale, and up and down the valley roosters were crow-
ing. Then Dan's ears caught another sound—the muffled, rapid thud of a horse's hooves on turf. He ran out
into the cold air and stood for a second, getting his
bearings. There it came again—out beyond the apple
orchard. Two fields away a horse, galloping fast, cleared
a stone wall with its dark-cloaked rider, and disappeared
in the woods beyond. But in that fleeting instant, Dan
thought he caught a flash of white as the horse's heels
lifted to the jump. "One white stocking," the squire
had said!

Still scared and shaken, the boy went back into the
barn and picked up the useless pistol. He could not have
fallen asleep again if he had tried—not after what had
happened. When, around sunrise, the supporters of law
and order began to straggle into the yard, he was wide
awake and decidedly glad to see them.

Chasing robbers was thirsty work, it appeared. No

sooner had Skilly Bassett gotten back to the inn than all members of the posse who were on hand swarmed into the keeping-room and surrounded the bar. For an hour or more they stayed there drinking and talking, till the last search-party had been heard from. There was no news. Not a vestige of the highwayman had any of them seen. That much Dan gathered from the scraps of conversation he picked up around the yard.

With some hesitation he had told Tim Garrity of his own experience. The hostler roared with laughter when he heard how the pistol had gone off. But he shook his head and grinned unbelievingly at the idea of the robber's having crossed the tavern fields.

"Belikes ye was still dreamin'," he told the boy. "Phwat wud he be comin' back here for, an' the whole wide county to hide in? Then ag'in, mebbe ye *was* awake, an' 'twas a deer ye saw. When they jump ye kin see the white tails of 'em."

After that Dan kept his own counsel, but he knew what he had seen. And all day, as he worked about the place, his eye kept straying toward that stretch of stone wall and the growth of scrub pine beyond it. Some time in the afternoon, when the down stage had departed and there were no more immediate chores to be done, he left the barn and hurried out across the withered stubble.

At first he found nothing. Then, two or three yards from the wall, he came on a horse-shoe print in the half-frozen ground. It was a blurred, imperfect mark, but it satisfied him, in his own mind at least. Climbing over the wall, he continued his search in the stony, brush-grown pasture. There was a fresh scar on an outcropping bit of granite just beyond the wall, but hunt as he would he could find nothing more. Which direction the rider had taken after crossing the wall remained a mystery.

.   .   .   .

It was a cold night, and still—a good night to sleep. Bone-tired from his activities of the night before, Dan turned in early and slumbered undisturbed till Tim called him at five. There was a skim of ice on the horse-trough under the pump that morning. By sunrise crows were cawing in the pasture, as they gathered in great flocks for their southward flight. There was a threat of winter in the biting air.

Just as Dan was finishing his after-breakfast chores, a shrill, cheerful whistle sounded outside the barn. He went to the door and saw young Ethan Hayes standing in the yard, grinning at him. The redhead had two guns under his arm—a handsome fowling-piece and an old long-barreled musket. Beside him frisked a big black and white mongrel dog.

"Hi, Dan," said Ethan. "This here's my dog, Rumpus. He's smart, spite of his looks. Part collie an' part English setter, but when there's guns around he thinks he's all bird-dog. We come to see 'f ye could git off to go huntin'."

Dan shook his head. "I sure would like to, but I've never asked Skilly fer anything like that—"

"All the more reason," the other boy interrupted. "Here—let me talk to him!"

He led the way to the tavern door and entered, with Dan close at his heels.

"Mr. Bassett," Ethan addressed the inn-keeper, "how'd ye like some nice fat pa'tridges to give the stage-passengers fer supper?" Then, before there was time for a reply—"I know where there's flocks of 'em, an' I thought if ye could spare Dan fer a few shakes, we'd go git ye some!"

The landlord's lips made a thin line as he polished a big flip-glass. "Tryin' to take boys away from their work, be ye? Why ain't ye in school this mornin'?"

" 'Cause it's Saturday," returned Ethan in triumph. "Them pa'tridges'll taste awful good, Mr. Bassett. He can come, can't he?"

"Yeah—I guess so," the inn-keeper grumbled. "But see the wood-boxes are filled first, an' be sure ye git back 'fore the down stage comes in."

Flying at the task together, the two boys made quick work of the wood-carrying. Then they set out with the dog across the fields. Ethan handed Dan the musket with its powder flask and bullet pouch.

"You used to guns?" he asked.

"I've shot one a few times," Dan replied. "Killed a gray squirrel once in Portsmouth. But I've never aimed at anything flyin'."

He chuckled to himself then, and told his companion the story of the pistol.

"Say!" exclaimed Ethan, with a whistle. "Think ye really saw him goin' over the wall? Golly, wish I'd been there! Mebbe they'd believe the two of us. But listen— if it *was* him, what d'ye s'pose he was doin' back here in the village?"

"That's what I've been tryin' to figger out," Dan said. "No reason I know of, unless he's got a hidin'-place somewhere off in the woods. If that's it, he might've doubled back knowin' the men were all scattered out on the different roads."

They had crossed the stone wall and Dan showed his friend the scarred rock on the other side.

"Yep," Ethan nodded. "That's just the kind o' mark an iron shoe makes. He must've come this way."

At that moment Rumpus, who had cruised off among the jack-pines, gave a low growl.

"Sh-h!" whispered Ethan. "He sees somethin'!"

They stole through the scattered trees and saw the dog standing at rigid attention.

"P'intin'!" breathed the farm boy. "Watch, now!"

He lifted his gun and stepped softly forward. When he was only a stride from the dog, several ruffed grouse went up from the thicket ahead with a deafening whirr. Ethan took quick aim and fired. "Got him!" he cried gleefully, and in a moment Rumpus was bounding back with the bundle of gray-brown feathers in his mouth.

"Didn't I tell ye he was all bird-dog?" laughed Ethan. "Here, keep close an' there'll be some more in a minute. You take the next shot while I'm loadin'."

They prowled forward, keeping an eye on the ranging dog. Soon he made another point, and Dan raised the long-barreled gun. He was trying not to be nervous, but the heavy piece wobbled in spite of everything. Then, so close it startled him, a partridge went roaring out of a pine-clump.

"*Bang!*" The old musket made a terrific report and kicked so hard that Dan fell backward into a juniper bush. Ethan laughed and gave him a hand up.

"That wa'n't bad," he said. "Didn't miss by much. I saw where the charge went, through that branch, just to the right of him. Load up an' try again."

In the next hour they put up several more birds, and

on his second attempt Dan was lucky enough to kill one. Ethan meanwhile had added two more to the bunch hanging from his shoulder.

Loading the long-barreled gun was a job that took time, and while Dan was still working with the ram-rod, Ethan hurried off to overtake the dog.

Dan started after him several minutes later. They were in thicker woods now and there was no trail to indicate which way he had gone. However the boy moved onward, expecting to hear a shot at any moment and get his bearings from that. He must have gone a quarter of a mile, listening at every step, before he thought of giving Ethan a hail. He shouted then, at the top of his lungs, but the only sound that came back was the whisper of the wind in the pine branches.

Dan felt no worry about getting lost, but he did want to rejoin his chum. Shouldering the heavy gun, he walked on, keeping the direction as well as he was able.

Ahead of him the trees seemed to be thinning. In a few moments he came out in a roughly cleared field, where corn stubble showed among the rocks and stumps. A small, unpainted house and a ramshackle barn stood near the middle of the clearing, and there was a lazy curl of wood-smoke rising from the chimney.

Perhaps Ethan had gone in to get a drink, thought Dan. He threaded his way between the stumps and approached the building. When he was a dozen yards from the door, a tremendous sound of barking arose, and suddenly two big brindled dogs, part mastiff from the look of them, came tearing toward him around the corner.

Dan stood his ground as they circled him, growling. While he was still undecided what to do, the door opened and the biggest woman he had ever seen stood there, hands on her hips, glaring down at him. She filled the doorway from top to bottom and from side to side. Over six feet tall she must have been, with unkempt, sandy hair, and ugly features, deep-lined now by her scowl.

"Be off with ye!" she roared.

Her voice was deep—almost as deep as a man's—and strangely hoarse. It was accompanied by a ferocious gesture of her huge, muscular arm.

It was quite apparent that Ethan wouldn't be found here.

"Yes'm," said Dan, politely, and took his way back to the woods as fast as he could move without actually running. The two mean-looking dogs continued to growl at his heels all the way to the edge of the clearing. There he picked up a stone as big as his fist and sent them yelping home. Five minutes later, heading back the way he had come, he heard the welcome voice of Ethan hallooing for him.

"Gosh, Dan, I thought ye'd got yerself lost!" exclaimed the farm boy when he came in sight. "I should ha' waited, back there. Where ye been?"

Dan told him, and described the giantess who had driven him off her premises.

Ethan's eyes opened wide. "She's a bad 'un to run afoul of," he said. "That's Big Liz—Big Liz Nixon!"

SIX

THE two boys worked back through the woods and rough pasture-land toward the tavern, two miles away. As they went Ethan told Dan what he knew about the Nixons. It was little enough, for the self-respecting farm and village folk gave the Nixon clearing a wide berth as a rule.

"They're newcomers," he said. "Been here only a couple o' years, anyhow. Nobody knows jest where they come from—somewheres south, I've heard—down Boston way. Most folks thinks the husband—Newt Nixon —must've done somethin' pretty bad an' come up here to hide out. He's a big feller himself, but don't look it, 'longside of his wife. Anyway he don't do a hand's turn of honest work, fur's the neighbors know. An' yet—it's a funny thing—he 'most always has a good team o' hosses. Might be a pair o' blacks this week an' roans the next. Some says he's a trader. Others—well, ye hear folks hint at queer goin's-on."

"You mean maybe he's a hoss-thief?" asked Dan in an

awed whisper, for he knew that horse-stealing ranked second only to murder in the list of serious crimes.

"I ain't sayin'," replied Ethan darkly. "But it's strange enough, ain't it? Nixon always seems to have plenty o' money, too."

They put up several more coveys of partridges on the way home, and though Dan's shooting still lacked a good deal of equaling the farm boy's, he did bring down another one. They had a total of six when they climbed the wall at the edge of Bassett's farm—all plump, full-grown birds as big as broiler chickens.

"All I want's a couple fer our house," said Ethan generously. "You give the rest to Skilly—that'll make him feel better about lettin' ye off again, mebbe."

It turned out that he was right. At least, when Dan entered the keeping-room and held up his four fat grouse, the landlord's face actually broke into a smile.

"That's fine, Danny," he said. "Go git yer dinner now. I ain't sure, but I guess Maria saved a bite fer ye. An' move quick, 'cause the stage'll likely be in 'fore ye've et."

In the kitchen Mrs. Bassett eyed the birds without enthusiasm. "They're a lot o' trouble fer the meat ye git off 'em," she remarked. "Still," she added grudgingly, "the city folks seem to set store by pa'tridge meat. I'll cook 'em an' put 'em on fer supper. Come, boy, why are ye standin' round? Don't ye see that plate o' vittles Kate kept warm fer ye?"

The pale sunlight that had been in evidence that morning was gradually obliterated by a harsh gray curtain of cloud. By nightfall there was a wind blowing, chill and sullen, from the east. The neighbors and freight-wagon men who gathered around the bar after supper were blowing on cold fingers and cursing the weather. With his evening chores out of the way, Dan came in to sit for a while in the corner by the great fireplace. He liked to watch the red flames and listen to the talk of the teamsters.

There was plenty of demand for Skilly Bassett's famous flip that night. The inn-keeper made it by his own recipe, beating cream and eggs to a froth, mixing them with warm ale and a dash of rum, and bringing the concoction to steaming heat by plunging into each glass the iron loggerhead, kept cherry red in the coals. The flip glasses themselves were huge affairs, holding upwards of a quart, and when a man drained one it warmed him to his toes.

A great deal of good-natured joking went on among the drinkers. "Look ye, Mose," one of the local farmers addressed a great barrel of a man who had come in with a freight-wagon, "I ain't sure whether that's three glasses o' flip ye've put away, or four. Better keep count.

Skilly might fergit to mark one down an' ye'd be cheatin' him!"

"Ho—ho!" bellowed the wagoner. "Whoever heard of a tavern-keeper bein' cheated! Puts me in mind of a

good'un they tell on the landlord down to Ashuelot Village—feller name o' Raymond. He's known as a mighty sharp business man, but a leetle short on readin' an' writin'. 'Long with his inn he keeps a sort o' store fer the farmers 'round about. One customer'd been runnin' a bill fer quite a spell, an' when he'd sold his hogs in the fall, he dropped in to pay up.

"Ol' Raymond stood there figgerin' out what had been bought an' callin' off the items one by one. Everythin' sounded all right till he come to the last paper, at the bottom o' the pile. 'An' one cheese,' he says. 'That's fourteen shillin'.'

" 'Cheese!' says the customer. 'I never bought no cheese from you. We make our own! Lemme see that paper.'

" 'Ye bought it, all right,' Raymond tells him. 'Look —here 'tis set down plain,' an' he points to a round circle. 'That's my mark fer a cheese.'

" 'Hm,' the other chap says, scratchin' his head, 'seems like I recollect one thing ye ain't charged me fer, an' that's a grind-stun.'

" 'What!' says ol' Raymond. 'Well, I snum! That there *is* a grind-stun, sure 'nough—only durned if I didn't fergit to put the hole in the middle!' "

Out of the chorus of chuckles came Skilly Bassett's peevish voice. "Why—" he said, horrified—"the ol' fool purty nigh lost himself money! A grind-stun's wuth twenty shillin' in any man's store!"

At that, the chuckles turned into roars of laughter. Another of the wagon-men leaned down to the fire and picked up the red-hot loggerhead, which hissed as he thrust it into his drink.

" 'Tain't very often," he said, "that anybody gits the

best of a Yankee inn-keeper. They're pushed purty close by the drovers, though. Ever hear the yarn about Uncle Cal Tenney, that kep' the halfway house 'tween Jaffrey an' Marlboro?

"Seems there come a drover through there with a big herd o' cattle. He turned 'em into Tenney's pasture fer the night an' ordered supper an' beds fer his men. In the mornin' he paid his board bill an' asked how much the pasturage 'mounted to. 'Two cents a head,' says Uncle Cal. 'How many cattle did ye bring?'

" 'A hundred an' twenty-five,' the drover answers, real prompt, an' slaps the money down. Uncle Cal don't say nothin'—jest takes it an' strolls out to the pasture bars, where the herd is startin' to come out. He counts up to a hundred an' twenty-five, then begins to put up the bars.

" 'Hey! What ye doin'?' hollers the drover. 'Let my cattle out!'

" '*Your* cattle?' Uncle Cal asks, surprised-like. 'Your hundred an' twenty-five's there in the road. These must be mine.' An' it wa'n't till the drover had owned up, paid fer the extry seventy-five head an' bought drinks fer the house, that he was 'lowed to drive his two hundred cattle off!"

"Heh, heh!" laughed Skilly. "Outsmarted the drover-feller, didn't he? I'll hafter remember that 'un. Mebbe work it myself some time."

"You don't need no lessons, Skilly," chuckled a farmer from up the East Hill. "Fix me one more glass o' flip, an' I've got to be gittin' home. Don't like to be gone at night with so many folks losin' hogs an' chickens."

"What's this?" the stocky freighter asked. "Trouble with thieves 'round here?"

The local man nodded soberly. "Three places robbed in the township last week."

"Who's doin' it? Don't they leave no traces?"

"No. If we should git a snow, mebbe they could be tracked, but so fur nobody has an idee who 'tis. I've been sleepin' with a gun handy, the last few nights."

One of the other neighbors slapped his fist down on the bar. "I've heard plenty o' folks say they 'spicioned who's the thief," he said darkly. "If ye ask me, I wouldn't look no further'n that good-fer-nothin' old Injun that hangs 'round."

"What! Ol' Gunticus?" replied the man from East Hill. "No, no, Sam! Why, I've knowed him fer twenty year. Made me a bow'n'arrer once when I was a little shaver. No—Gunticus may be shif'less but he don't steal hogs!"

At this the other farmer shook his head, unconvinced. "Never seen an Injun yit that wouldn't steal 'fore he'd work," he answered stubbornly. "Mark my words—they'll ketch the rascal sooner or later."

Dan had listened to this clash of opinions with a good deal of interest. Once or twice, in the month he had spent at the Fox and Stars, he had seen the old Indian about the place. Gunticus, Tim had told him, was the last surviving relic of a tribe once powerful in the Contoocook valley. He would slip silently into the tavern room, buy a little tobacco or a dram of cheap rum, and depart without speaking half a dozen words.

A dirty, unkempt old man, wearing ragged clothes he had made himself, he still preserved a certain dignity. His face was deep-lined, an impassive mask the color of weathered oak. No one seemed to know just where he lived. "Belikes it's in some cave o' rocks, back on the mountain," had been the hostler's guess.

The wagon-men began to spread their great-coats on the sanded floor, and the farmers paid for their flip and made ready to leave. Dan went out to his bed in the barn. As he crossed the yard the wind buffeted him and cold particles stung his cheeks. The first snow of winter had begun.

   . . .

In the morning the wind had died, and the level beams of a pink sunrise glistened on a blanket of snow four or five inches deep. The air was clear and bracing.

As Dan thawed out the pump and drew water for the teams, he could hear sounds of cheerful activity coming from other farms the whole breadth of the valley. The cackle of hens and the neighing of horses; the squealing complaint of a barn door being opened; the musical *ker-lunk, ker-lunk* of other pump handles vigorously worked.

Rising before dawn, he had already shoveled out a path for the stage passengers to use in going from the tavern door to the coach. Then there had been wood to carry for the breakfast fires, and the usual stable chores. There was plenty of exercise to keep him warm despite the sharp chill of the morning.

The big freight teams lumbered out of the yard, straining and slipping, the broad wagon-tires making a singing sound in the crisp snow. The drivers were glum, for they knew they would have trouble making their mileage that day.

By mid-morning a few of the villagers had sleighs out, and the jingle of bells came pleasantly up the hill. But the coaches were still on wheels. When the down stage got in that afternoon, a full hour late, there were solid chunks of snow between the wheel-spokes, and the panting horses were lathered white.

Tim Garrity hummed a plaintive Irish ditty as he and Dan rubbed down the tired team. "It ain't so bad," he said, "after winter starts in earnest. Then ye'll see iverybody slidin' along on runners. The mean time fer the horses is at the beginnin'—what wid little snow-storms like this."

"Tell me," said Dan, whose mind had been on a different subject, "do you think the old Injun, Gunticus, would steal pigs an' hens?"

"Maybe—an' him hungry enough," the Irishman replied lightly. "Ye niver can tell what a man'll do whin the pinch is on him. So it's thim stories ye've been puzzlin' yer head over, eh? An' belikes ye've been thinkin' 'tis our bould, bad highwayman himself is in it?"

He laughed. "No, no, Danny! He's too much the gintleman to soil his white hands wid a pig!"

Dan flushed. Ever since the night of Squire Pierce's robbery and its thrilling aftermath, he had been the butt of Tim's good-humored joking. It wasn't the dark-cloaked rider he suspected of these barnyard thefts. But for the present he resolved to say no more about it.

That night the supper had to be kept warm till hours after the usual arrival of the stage. When the weary travelers finally stamped into the dining-room it was close to ten and long past Dan's bed-time. Yawning and stumbling, he helped Garrity put up the horses. Just before the hostler took his lantern from its peg he let fall a remark that made Dan's sleepy eyes snap open.

"Nate Gilman, the stage-driver, was tellin' me he'd brought handbills from Boston," Tim said. "Description of a highway robber, an' offerin' a money reward fer puttin' him behind bars. Ye'll be wantin' to take a look at it in the mornin', I'm thinkin'. Good-night, lad."

The boy snuggled down in the hay, his nerves a-tingle with excitement. He had half a mind to go to the keeping-room at once and see if the handbill had been posted. Then he remembered how late it was. Skilly would surely have gone to bed and left the wagoners to their night's rest by this time. Reluctantly he closed his eyes—and before he knew it Garrity's lantern was shining in his face again. It was morning.

As soon as the chores were done and breakfast eaten, Dan hurried to the big front room of the tavern. Four or five men were standing before a paper, tacked to the wall, laboriously spelling out its printed message. Dan squeezed near enough to see for himself.

At the top was a stilted woodcut of a galloping horse with a hatted and cloaked rider. Then, under the bold letters of the word "REWARD!!" appeared several paragraphs of smaller type.

"*Whereas*: there is now at large a notorious Robber, known by the name of Capt. Hairtrigger and by divers other names, and,

"*Whereas*: the said Capt. Hairtrigger has committed sundry dastardly Crimes against the Citizens, and in the Commonwealth, of Massachusetts; namely: robbing Josiah Bigelow, of Waltham, of a sum of Money at the Pistol's point; stealing a fast and well-broke bay saddle Horse from Eliphalet Adams, of Lexington; making off with 2 sacks of Mail from the post-house of William Savage, on the Newburyport Turnpike, and other like Depradations; therefore,

"*Be it resolved*: that all good Citizens of the States of Massachusetts, New Hampshire, Vermont, Connecticut, and of other Parts wherever the said Capt. Hairtrigger may be Practicing his Nefarious Deeds, shall make an Effort toward his Apprehension and Speedy Conviction. And further,

"*Be it resolved*: that for information leading to such Apprehension, this Society offers a Reward of 100 Dollars Gold, to be paid as soon as the said Capt. Hairtrigger may be fast in Gaol.

"When last seen, near Danvers, Capt. Hairtrigger was riding a very fine black Horse, and was wearing a blue Cloak and Beaver Hat. He is of a Tall and slender Figure, about 5 foot 11 in. or 6 foot. Bears on the forehead branded Letters, H.T., put upon him when he was earlier apprehended in Connecticut, and after Escaped.

"Beware of this Robber, who is both Resolute and well Armed!!"

Oct. 13, 1827   *The Danvers Thief Detecting*
                                              Society

Ben Tucker, the burly smith, was the first of the men to finish reading the notice. He turned deliberately and sent a carefully aimed spurt of tobacco juice into the box of sawdust in the corner.

"Hm!" he rumbled. "Fancy names these fellers like to give 'emselves! 'Cap'n Hairtrigger,' eh? I'd like to git one crack at him with my sledge, an' see if he's so all-fired quick on the trigger!"

"Think he's the man tried to rob Skilly's till?" a neighbor inquired.

"Dunno—I wa'n't here that night," said Tucker. "But it sounds as if it might be. You seen him, boy. What's your jedgment?"

Dan was a little flustered by the question but he spoke up. "Yes," he said. "I b'lieve it's the same man— an' the one that got the squire's watch an' money, too."

"Well," boasted one of the farmers who had been out with the constable's posse, "if it's that feller we won't have to worry 'bout him in this neck o' the woods. Way we chased him, t'other night, he'll want to give Deptford a wide berth. Come on, Ben—my mare's waitin' to be shod an' the mornin's half gone a'ready."

SEVEN

AS he went about the day's round of work, Dan kept turning over the words of the handbill in his mind. October 13th, it had been dated. That was just about the time he came to the tavern. He wasn't sure of the exact day, but he knew it had been near the middle of October. As he recalled the swift galloping of the black horse, coming over the hill in the dusk, and tried to reconstruct his impressions of that moment, one thing was clear in his memory. "Whoever's coming," his first thought had been, "he's running away from something!"

Running away. From Massachusetts? Where he had last been seen—sometime shortly before the 13th of October—riding a fine black horse and wearing a cloak and beaver hat? The facts dovetailed too perfectly to leave room for doubt.

Dan took the silver dollar out of his breeches pocket and looked at it curiously. A present from Captain Hairtrigger, the notorious highwayman. It gave him a shivery feeling! And in spite of the confident belief of the village that the robber had been scared away, the boy could not help wondering whether he had seen the last of that lonely rider.

The snow that had fallen stayed on the ground only two days. Under a strangely warm November sun it melted fast, leaving all the roads except the stone-surfaced turnpike deep and treacherous with mud.

Farmers who came to the inn cursed volubly at the weather. "Bad enough to haul through mud in the spring," they said. " 'Tain't reasonable to have it in fall, too!"

Then, as the hot, clear days continued through a week of true Indian summer, the mud dried up and the roads grew passable again. Dan enjoyed the balmy air. It was so delightfully mild that he was half tempted to get Ethan Hayes and go for a swim in the river.

Loungers around the tavern told queer tales of wild flowers sprouting in the woods, and maple trees starting to bud. One man even swore he had heard a frog peeping, down in the marsh below the town. "Mebbe we ain't goin' to git no winter at all this year," was a comment frequently heard.

To such remarks Skilly Bassett replied with a snort. "You fellers better be luggin' in extry wood fer yer fires an' sewin' ear-flaps on yer fur caps," he cautioned.

84

"Any time we have onnat'ral weather, ye kin bet it'll be made up fer, later. I got a feelin' in my bones that 'fore very long now we'll ketch weather to make yer hair curl!"

But as the days drew on toward Thanksgiving, the valley still basked in lazy warmth. Cattle stood out in the pasture lanes all day long, chewing their cuds under the naked elms as if it were midsummer.

Dan wondered, with a twinge of homesickness, what the feast-day would be like, here at the inn. The Bassetts, he knew, were driving down to Jaffrey to spend the holiday with relatives. He and Tim, he supposed, would take what the hired girls cooked for them, and work as usual.

He was due for a pleasant surprise. On Tuesday, as soon as school was out, Ethan came panting up to the inn, his freckled face beaming.

"Hey, Dan!" he called. "Ma says I kin have ye over fer Thanksgivin' dinner! Will ye come?"

Would he come! Together, the boys went in to beard Skilly in his den. The landlord was in a rare good humor. "Yes, yes—I know," he grinned at them. "I seen Mrs. Hayes this mornin'. All right, Danny, soon's the mornin' chores is over ye kin go. Tim won't need ye to handle the down stage. An' there won't be any other teams stoppin', to speak of."

So it happened that on Thanksgiving morning Dan scrubbed himself with extra care, brushed the dust out of his blue jacket, and even borrowed some harness-polish to shine his work boots. At ten he set off down the road to the church, where he was to meet Ethan.

The yard in front of the stately white building was filled with villagers and farm-folk in their Sunday best. He spied his young friend through the crowd and went to join him. Just as he got there a voice spoke at his shoulder.

"Hello, Dan Drew!" It was Molly Crandall, her mischievous dark eyes atwinkle. "I hear we're both going to Cousin Ethan's for dinner," she said.

"You—you're his cousin?" asked Dan, abashed. "I didn't know *you'd* be there."

"Well!" She tossed her head and laughed. "It looks like you don't think much of the idea!"

Dan reddened uncomfortably. "Oh, no!" he blurted. "It ain't that! I was just wishin' I had some better clothes—"

"Here he is," Ethan interrupted at that moment. "Come on, Dan. Folks are goin' in. You come sit in our pew. Say—has that tomboy been plaguin' you? Gals are all born teases, anyhow. Shoo, Molly! Go on an' leave us menfolks to ourselves!"

Dan had not been to church since coming to Dept-

ford, and many of the congregation stared at him between hymns and during the sermon. The service was
shorter than on Sundays, the minister explaining that

he knew some of the women wanted to get back to their
cooking. He preached only about an hour, instead of
the two or more hours that were customary.

By noon the crowd was outside again, exchanging
greetings, unhitching the horses from the long, half-

open sheds, and clambering into the carriages.

Five Hayeses and Dan squeezed in on the two seats of their light wagon and Ethan's father touched up the team. Followed by the Crandalls, they trotted up the dusty road to the farm on the hill.

From the start, Dan felt at home with Ethan's family. They were plain, prosperous farm people, used to hard work and boisterous good times. There were two other children besides Ethan—a well-grown lad of nineteen, named Elijah, and a spry, sandy-haired ten-year-old girl, generally called "Sis." It was not until long after that Dan learned her proper name was Hepsibah.

As soon as they reached the farm the women and girls put on big aprons and rushed to the kitchen. The menfolks, including Dan and Ethan, went outside to talk and whittle and stroll about the buildings, looking at the stock. Ethan showed his friend the pair of young steers he was breaking to the yoke, and the traps he was going to set for skunks and foxes as soon as snow came.

At two o'clock Molly Crandall hallooed from the kitchen door and they all went in to dinner.

Dan thought he had seen bountiful tables before, but never one to compare with this. Even the harvest supper at the inn was surpassed by the array of food Mrs. Hayes had set forth. The turkey must have weighed thirty pounds at least. It was so big that Jonathan

Hayes' perspiring face only appeared from behind it at intervals while he carved. And the vegetables—the jellies and conserves—the fragrant, steaming pies—mince, apple and pumpkin! It looked enough to feed an army.

When they had eaten all they could hold and helped wash the dishes, the youngsters went out to play hide-and-seek in the great, hay-filled barn till dusk. Then a lamp was lighted in the parlor and everybody gathered about the wheezy little organ for a sing. Molly played, pumping valiantly on the pedals and getting all the music out of the rheumatic instrument that was possible to human fingers. They started with hymn-tunes, then went on to such old, familiar songs as "Drink to me only with thine eyes," and "Charlie is my darling."

Dan liked to sing. His voice had changed the year before, and he was just discovering that he had a true and fairly strong baritone. He enjoyed himself that evening.

At nine o'clock good-nights were said. Dan knew his manners, and went bashfully to shake hands with Mrs. Hayes. "I sure had a fine time, ma'am," he told her. "You an' Ethan are mighty good to me."

She put a motherly arm around him and brushed the sudden moisture from her cheek with the corner of her apron.

"Why, Dan, we like to have ye here," she said. "Come

over again—jest as soon as Skilly'll let ye!"

He was given a lift in the Crandalls' carry-all as far as the turnpike, and climbed the hill to the Fox and Stars with a singing heart. Once again he had that peaceful sense of being in a place where he belonged.

.   .   .

For another day the weather held clear and mild. Then came a haze of low clouds and sultry, windless stillness. The smoke from the tavern chimneys hung all day like a blanket, and there were low, distant rumblings of thunder around the gray horizon.

" 'Tain't right nor fittin', this time o' year," Skilly Bassett's querulous voice complained. "I'm satisfied somethin's a-comin'. Tim, I want ye to see everythin's battened down tight tonight. From the way that weathervane keeps backin' an' fillin' I reckon we'll have a storm o' wind 'fore mornin'."

Leaving the tavern room at bedtime, Dan noticed a sudden chill in the air and heard shutters rattling. There were no stars overhead. The black night had begun to moan with a restless, prowling wind. Shivering, the boy hurried to the barn and closed and barred the big door. Inside all was warm and quiet. He pulled off his boots and jacket, spread the blanket and burrowed into the hay.

Several times in the night Dan was half-wakened by

a roaring, swishing noise. Once he started up convulsively from a dream, thinking the barn was on fire. A frightened glance about him showed no leaping flames, but there was plenty going on outside, as he could hear. Groping his way to the door he tried to peer through a narrow crack, and felt against his face the cold of snowflakes sifting in on a fierce blast of air. A blizzard! But there was nothing he could do about it. He went back to his blanket and slept till morning.

At six o'clock—a full hour later than usual—Tim Garrity came out through the sheds to the barn. His face was sober in the light of the lantern. "The stage won't be goin' out today," he told Dan, "so I gave ye a bit of extra slape. 'Tis such a storm as ye niver seen, I'll be bound. An' if anny poor sowl was on the road last night, may the howly saints have pity on 'em! Git into yer boots, now. We'll have to be shovelin' a path to the pump."

With both their shoulders against the door they succeeded in wedging it open a crack. In the screaming smother outside it was hardly possible to see a man's length. Even the nearby sheds vanished and reappeared in flying swirls of white.

"This way! Stick close to me, lad!" yelled the Irishman, and together they attacked the first drift with their shovels. Though both worked like mad it took them nearly half an hour to dig the forty feet to the pump. When they had cleared the snow out around it, Dan hurried back through their trench to bring out a kettle of hot water. The walls of snow rose higher than his head in places, and the tortured wraiths of the storm danced along the edges, threatening to drift the tunnel full before it could be used.

The boy had been too busy to notice the cold, but when he reached the kitchen he found his fingers were so numb he could barely move them. Maria Bassett saw him trying to thaw his hands by blowing on them and snapped out an order to one of the girls. "Ye'll find 'em on my dresser, Kate," she said. "An old pair o' Skilly's that I jest finished darnin'. Come—move fast!"

By the time the steaming kettle was ready, Kate had returned with a pair of thick, red wool mittens. "Put 'em on, boy! What ye standin' there fer?" barked the landlady.

Back at the pump, a few dousings of the boiling water freed the ice from the plunger, and Dan was soon carrying buckets of water to the horses.

When he went in to breakfast he found the coachman and half a dozen west-bound travelers marooned by the blizzard. Some of the latter were taking their enforced sojourn badly—pacing the floor, scowling at their watches and staring through the windows at the blind scurry of the snow. A few had joined plump Nate Gilman, the driver, in making the best of the situation. Dan could hear their laughter and the clink of their glasses coming from the keeping-room.

All day he kept the big fires roaring. Even so the biting cold stole in through the walls of the house and crept

along the floors. When evening came, some of the lady guests complained that the water-pitchers in the upstairs chambers were filled with solid ice. Sue and Kate were kept on the run from the first floor to the second, carrying big brass warming-pans full of coals to heat the beds. And still it snowed.

Dan went to sleep again that night to the howl of the storm. He had become so accustomed to it that when he woke at daybreak and heard nothing it frightened him for a moment. The silence was heavy—almost oppressive. Tim had not yet appeared, and without the lantern it was dark in the barn. However, Dan succeeded in forcing the door open far enough to let him peep outside. Under the fading stars lay a strangely deformed world of white. Drifts like mountain ranges covered the yard higher than the fences, and billowed above the sills of the tavern windows.

In spite of the absence of wind the cold was still intense. Dan buttoned his jacket tight, pulled on his cap and mittens, and started shoveling. By the time the hostler showed up, he had made a fine start on the tunnel to the pump.

"Good lad!" shouted Tim encouragingly. "But we'll have to dig it wider—wide enough to let the coach through."

"You mean they'll try to get out today?" Dan exclaimed. "Why, it must be ten foot deep, some places on the road!"

"Ye'll see the plows by mid-day," replied Tim. "An' if we're not past the elm trees wid our path we'll be houldin' up the United States mails."

Dan could hardly believe him, but he pitched in with a will. By sun-up the coachman had joined them and the broad trench pushed steadily out toward the turnpike. They stopped long enough for breakfast. Nate Gilman straightened up from his shoveling with a groan, and wiped the sweat from his round, red face. "Ridin' the box don't put ye in very good shape fer this sort of a job!" he grinned ruefully. "I'm sure goin' to 'preciate my vittles, though!"

Tim was right about the village plows. The path was barely open as far as the road when they heard boys shouting, down the hill, and saw the ox-teams wallowing through the drifts.

That was a picture Dan wouldn't soon forget. Six yoke of great, slow-footed beasts pulled the first plow. There was something tremendous about their tireless advance. Patiently, yard by yard, they rammed their way through snow that came half way up their steaming sides. Boys and men—as many as could hang on—rode the plows to keep them down. And the shouting drivers floundered along, guiding the teams by voice and goad.

As they hauled up abreast of the tavern, the contagion of the struggle caught Dan and he raced in, asking the landlord's permission to go with them.

"Git the stage off first," Skilly told him. "Then, if they kin use another hand, I've no objection."

The boy helped Tim put the horses in harness, and in a few minutes the coach was pulling out. Nate Gilman waved his whip to them. "Dunno how fur I'll git," he called cheerfully, "but if all the towns is as smart as

Deptford, we'll make out fine."

Dan hurried out to the road. There was still nearly a foot of snow left in the great trench dug by the plows, but he pushed forward at a jog-trot, eager to overtake them. The straining oxen had made two or three hundred yards since passing the inn, and were nearing the crest of the hill. Suddenly the loud geeing and hawing of the drivers ceased. There was a confused babble of voices, and the crews left their places on the plows to run forward.

As Dan came closer he saw that the leading team had stopped, part way through a great drift, and a dozen men with shovels were digging away the snow beside them. He passed the plows and the stolid-eyed cattle.

"Wait!" he heard someone shout. "There's a man here, beside the horse!"

With a sick feeling, the boy edged his way forward and tried to see. A youngster in front of him turned quickly, his eyes scared and his lips pale and trembling. "He's black!" he whispered in terror. "A black-faced man!"

The shovelers were pulling something out of the snow, carrying it back, stretching it on the wooden platform of the plow.

Dan had seen negroes from the coasting ships in Portsmouth town, and one glimpse told him that the frozen body was that of a colored man. It was a strangely peaceful face, staring up at the cold sky. Wrinkled ebony with a fringe of kinky gray beard. A frail, twisted body in threadbare, plum-colored livery.

Ben Tucker, the blacksmith, seemed to be in command of the plows. He bent over the old negro's breast for a moment and shook his head. "You, Zeke, an' John, an' Eben," he ordered, pointing to some of the bigger boys, "turn the last plow around an' haul this pore feller back to the tavern. The rest of us," he addressed the crews, "have got a job to do. That hoss is harnessed to pull double. Reckon ye all know what that means. The black man had cut him loose an' started to ride fer help. Back along the road somewheres there's a kerridge, an' mebbe folks in it. Come on, now—git those oxen movin'!"

EIGHT

DAN watched them swing the patient cattle and start down the hill with their grisly load. There was something horrible in the thought of that man and horse fighting through the blizzard. Past the crest of the hill they had come—perhaps even within sight of the lighted tavern windows. Then the awful floundering in the drift—exhaustion—helplessness—and the merciful release of the cold.

The boy shivered and ran to make a place for himself on the crowded platform of the second plow. Their progress was slow but steady. In places where the snow was deepest, the shovel-crews worked ahead of the oxen, clearing a foothold so that the powerful brutes could pull. In two hours they had made something over a mile and were close to the eastern boundary of the township.

One or two of the men wanted to turn back, saying they had their own chores to do, but Tucker silenced them. "By rights," he said, "the road from here on is a job fer the West Wilton plows. But this may be a matter o' life an' death. Let's keep on a spell further."

One of the advance shovelers was pointing ahead. "Look, Ben," he called, "ain't that somethin' stickin' up out o' the snow?"

There was, indeed, a dark object, crested over by the top of a drift, not fifty yards beyond the oxen.

"Hup in thar!" shouted the lead driver. "Gee over, Star! Haw, you, Buck!" And the plows went into motion. Ahead, the men dug furiously, plunging into shoulder-high snow and rapidly nearing their goal.

"It's a kerridge!" someone yelled excitedly. "Here's the nigh hoss—down acrost the pole!" Flying shovels pulled away the snow and gradually there appeared the shape of a four-wheeled traveling-chaise with a leather hood and a curtain fastened across the front. Dan saw them starting to cut away the curtain and a dread seized him. He turned away so that he would not see. But the voices told him.

"Froze solid," a man said in a hushed tone. "A shame, too—she's a handsome woman, an' young. Hold on! Look at this, Ben! Rolled up in this big fur robe, here!"

There was a moment of silence and then a shout. "By thunder, it's a baby—an' alive, too!"

Dan stumbled toward the carriage, surrounded now by a score of wondering men and boys.

Ben Tucker came shouldering through, with a bundle in his brawny arms. "Turn them oxen in a hurry!" he yelled. "Bring the woman on the plow. I'll carry the baby. If we git to the tavern in time, mebbe we kin save it."

He started off rapidly through the loose snow in the plow track. Dan had to trot to keep abreast of his stride. "Pore little mite!" the blacksmith was muttering, half to himself. "Must be nigh starved, let alone froze. Any man would let his wife and child set out travelin' in a storm like that oughta be shot! But, by gum, she done her durndest to save the little 'un! Wrapped it up in the bearskin an' put her own cloak over it. That's mother-love fer ye!"

Dan, still hurrying along at the smith's side, ventured to interrupt his soliloquy. "Mr. Tucker," he panted, "if you're gettin' tired, I'll carry the baby a spell—"

The big man looked at him in surprise, then gave him

an understanding grin. "No, Danny," he said. "This little thing ain't heavy. 'Sides, I'm 'fraid ye'd drop it. Come on, I'm goin' to run, now."

And run he did, making such speed through the snow that Dan could barely keep behind him. They reached the inn ahead of the others. Skilly Bassett and two or three customers were gathered around the fire. The colored man's body had been laid out in the shed to await the coming of the coffin-maker, and they were discussing the tragic happening in low voices.

"Here—" gasped Tucker, short of breath—"fetch Maria, quick. We got to save this baby."

Mrs. Bassett was on the scene in a few seconds, managing everything with sharp efficiency. "Ben," she snapped, "take the child in the parlor, 'way from the fire. Dan, fetch me a dishpan full o' snow, an' send the girls here. Out o' the way, the rest o' ye. This is a job fer womenfolks."

Dan brought the snow and set it down inside the door, then ran to the barn. In a few words he told Tim what they had found in the buried chaise. "The woman was past help," he finished, "but they're tryin' to save the baby. Don't ye think one of us ought to ride fer a doctor?"

Tim shook his head. "Old Doc Reynolds has been ailin' lately," he said. "He wouldn't be wantin' to stir out, an' it so cold. But I can tell ye, if there's half a chance, ye kin bet on Black Maria to pull the wee feller through."

Noon came and went but nobody thought of dinner. The men stood around the main room talking in whispers and waiting. When the woman's body had been laid beside that of her old servant in the wood-shed, Tim had tiptoed in for a look at her. He came back to the stable with a sad countenance.

"A beautiful face," he said soberly. "Dark an' lovely —from Spain, belikes—or the western islands. A wee rosary wid a gold cross 'round her neck, an' a fine gold marriage ring on her finger. Poor colleen, she's wid the saints now, rest her sowl!"

At two o'clock there was good news from the tavern-parlor. The landlord's wife emerged, her face grim with weariness but triumphant. "She'll live, all right," she announced. "It's a girl, 'bout three year old. Come to, a while back, an' called fer her ma, pore young 'un! Can't talk but a few words, but she says her name's 'Dolowes,' or some sech outlandish-soundin' thing. Furriners, I reckon. Mrs. Crandall's a-holdin' her in there now."

.   .   .

By the next morning, everybody in the village had heard the story of the tragedy. Luke Slade, the carpenter, who also acted as undertaker, came to the inn early and made measurements for the pine boxes he was to build. The local authorities, including Squire Pierce and the constable, made an official investigation of the clothing, the carriage and other belongings which had been found. In the woman's purse there was upwards of fifty dollars, but no papers or cards that might help in identifying her. The chaise was apparently a private one, for it was not marked with the name of any post-house or livery-stable. The only possible clue was a brass plate on one of the bridles, bearing the address of a harness-maker's shop in Baltimore. As soon as the squire was satisfied of these details he wrote letters to Boston and Baltimore asking for any information that could be given, and awaited an opportunity to post them.

For two more days, no stages came through from either direction. Nate Gilman, they heard, had suc-ceeded in getting as far as Keene but had been stopped there by the condition of the roads. It was not until the third morning after the storm that a loud jingling of bells was heard, and a queer-looking four-horse con-veyance came into the yard at a smart trot. Running out, Dan saw a long box-body mounted on front and rear sleds. It had a roof, held up by wooden braces, and curtains of cloth and leather completely shut in the after part. A driver's box was tacked on in front, over the forward sled.

"Come, lad!" laughed Tim Garrity. "Don't ye know a stage-coach whin ye see it? Step lively an' snatch out that lead-team."

The coachman climbed down stiffly from his perch, swinging his arms, for the temperature was still well below freezing. As soon as his numb fingers could operate the fastenings, he unbuttoned one of the side curtains and let his passengers alight. "Right into the tavern, folks!" he called jovially. "A big fire to warm ye, an' plenty o' hot flip to be had at the bar!"

He winked at Dan, as he followed the travelers toward the door. "Skilly'd ought to serve me on the house, arter a speech like that, eh, boy?" he said.

Opening the curtains for a peep into the "coach," the boy saw three board benches with low wooden backs, set crosswise in the sled body. The bottom was filled with loose hay to give the passengers' feet some protection from the cold. But even so, it looked far from comfortable.

That night the Deptford villagers held a special town-meeting to discuss what should be done about the victims of the blizzard. Dan was not there but he heard, in the morning, that it had been voted to give both the woman and the colored man burial in the local churchyard. Mrs. Crandall had asked permission to care for the baby, Dolores, until some word came from friends or relatives. And so the matter had been settled.

Early in the afternoon Dan saw the Crandalls' sleigh, drawn by a stocky little gray mare, come jogging up to the inn door. Molly and her mother got out.

"Here! Stable-boy!" called the girl imperiously. "Come and take care of the horse!"

He must have scowled as he obeyed her summons, for she burst into mischievous laughter. "Don't get mad, Dan Drew," she said. "I love to order people 'round, an' I don't often get such a chance. Just put the blanket on her and let her stand. We won't be long, I guess. Just came to get the baby."

Carrying in wood, a few minutes later, Dan found the women assembled in the kitchen. Maria Bassett was tying a knitted wool bonnet on the tiny orphan's head. "It's good o' ye to take her, Mis' Crandall," she said. "I reckon a tavern ain't no place to bring up a sweet little young 'un like this. Ye'll be able to give more time 'n I would to lookin' after her. But, my lands—" her harsh voice was perilously close to cracking and she made a quick wipe at her eye with a work-roughened hand— "I—I sort o' hate to see her go!"

Mrs. Crandall laid a sympathetic hand on the land-lady's shoulder. "There now," she answered, "don't you feel upset. I want you to come see her every chance you get. Goodness knows the poor baby mightn't have been alive if she hadn't had your care!"

Dan tiptoed closer for his first real view of little Dolores. In the circle of the woolen hood her face looked small and wistful. But what touched him most was her great long-lashed black eyes that stared gravely up at him. Molly knelt beside the child and pointed. "See the boy, honey? That's Dan. Can you say 'Dan'?"

"Dan?" spoke Dolores doubtfully, and the boy grinned in delight.

"Gee!" he murmured. "She really said my name!"

Mrs. Bassett noticed him for the first time. "Look at them boots!" she said accusingly. "Trackin' snow in my kitchen again. Scat!"

"We'll be coming in a minute, Dan," Molly called after him. "You might take the blanket off the horse."

He was standing by the gray mare's head when they came out. Dolores, in Mrs. Crandall's arms, gave a frightened look at the snow and the sleigh and began to cry as if her heart would break.

"Oh, the poor lamb!" Molly exclaimed. "She remembers. What'll we do, Mother?"

At that moment the mare shook herself and the sleigh-bells rang out melodiously. The sound acted like magic. Dolores' tears stopped flowing. She looked at the sleigh again, laughed and clapped her mittened hands.

"Do it a-den, Dan!" she demanded. And to the merry jingle of the bells, she set out for her new home.

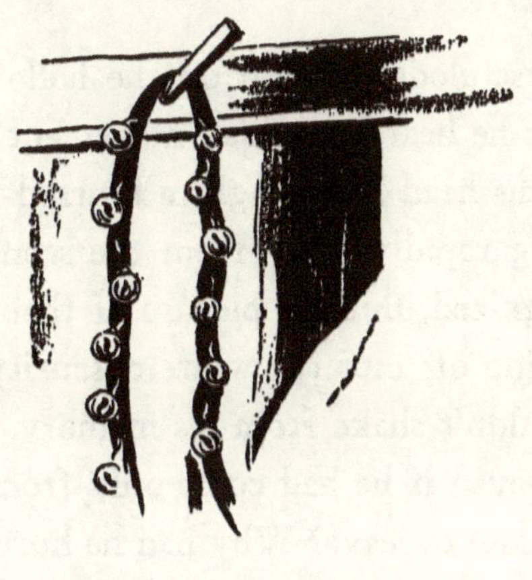

It was snowing hard next day when the funeral procession started slowly down the hill. Half a hundred sleighs and pungs had gathered at the tavern, for there was hardly a family in the township that was not stirred to pity. On a plain farm sled, drawn by a pair of work horses, lay the two pine coffins, stained with a crude mixture of soft soap and lampblack. Ben Tucker, his bearded head bare to the snow, held the reins and walked beside the team.

For hours that morning a volunteer crew of grave diggers had labored in the churchyard, clearing away the drifts and breaking the iron-hard ground.

Dan was deeply impressed by that bleak winter

burial. The brief and homely service. The silent crowd of sympathetic neighbors, half seen through the steadily falling snow.

As the first clods thudded on the hollow wood, the boy thought he heard a sudden movement behind him. He turned his head and caught a blurred glimpse of a man walking rapidly away from the scene. It was no one he recognized. But the picture of that tall, muffled figure, striding off into the white obscurity, was something he couldn't shake from his memory. Why should a stranger—even if he had come only from curiosity— be in such haste to leave? Why had he hurried off while all the others were still standing with bowed heads? Such questions came back to trouble Dan many times in the days and nights that followed.

NINE

BY the first week in December, a stretch of fair, cold weather had packed the roads hard and smooth. And with the good sleighing came an entirely new kind of traffic to throng the turnpike. The big 'stogy wagons were put up for the winter. The droves of cattle and sheep no longer moved in their slow clouds of dust. In their places appeared all manner of sledges, pungs and sleighs, drawn by from one to four horses.

Farmers from all the country round about, and even as far as northern Vermont, were hauling their goods to market. There must have been thousands of them on the roads between the Green Mountains and the sea. Often a dozen neighbors would make the trip together, their teams trailing in a long line, noisy with shouting and songs.

At that time of year there was little to do on the snowbound farms, and the men and boys welcomed the chance to go a-journeying.

Dan liked to watch them passing and he frequently

talked with them when they stopped to bait and water their horses. They had a queer assortment of names for their various rigs. The bigger sleds with two pairs of runners were generally called bob-sleds, or bobs. They carried heavy loads and it took four horses to get them through, if the pulling was bad. The commonest type of conveyance was a single sled with a box body and two horses, known as a "pod-auger."

In ordinary speech a pod-auger was a tool Dan had often seen used for boring holes in timbers. Its bit was an inch or more in diameter and it was turned by both hands on a wooden cross-bar at the top. Why the stout farm sleds were given this nick-name the boy never discovered, but so it was. And in similar fashion, the smallest one-horse sleds were called "gimlets." Travelers who were not hauling loads rode in light single-seated cutters or two-seated pungs.

The goods going to market were even more varied than the rigs themselves. All through the fall, the farmers and their wives had been busy preparing their products. There were butchered hogs, split and frozen; dressed chickens, ducks and turkeys; venison and bear meat; tubs of butter and great round cheeses; sacks of corn and peas and beans; raw wool and sheep pelts; hanks of homespun yarn; knitted stockings and mittens; hand-loomed cloth of wool or linen; hickory nuts gathered by the boys, and fox and mink skins that they had trapped. Anything and everything that could be sold at a profit in the city had been carefully harvested and worked into shape for this occasion.

When Dan first saw the roads swarming with these farm teams, he supposed the tavern would do an enormous business. There was indeed a good deal of traffic at the bar, but the dining-room was rarely filled. The thrifty farm lads carried their own food and provender. On each sled was a supply of oats for the horses and a big chest called a "mitchin-box," holding enough food to last the whole journey. Bean porridge, frozen in a huge, solid chunk, was one of the staples. It could be chopped off with an ax, and warmed over a roadside fire. Then there was cold roast pork, "rye-an'-injun" bread, cheese, sausages and doughnuts.

At night the barn was filled with horses and the travelers lay packed like herring on the floor of the keeping-room.

Dan enjoyed the bustle of those days. The work had hardened him and he had gained both height and breadth since coming to the inn. He was almost as big as Tim Garrity now, and able to hold his own with the Irishman in their occasional friendly tussles. He missed the visits with Silas Penny, but he made new acquaintances among the pod-auger men each day, and found them jolly enough company.

One evening just at dusk, he was on his way to the tavern room when he saw a shadowy figure coming across the field. The snow lay three feet deep on the level but this man was walking easily over its surface. As he approached, Dan saw that he was wearing snowshoes, and was wrapped in a ragged blanket. It was old Gunticus, the Indian.

"Evening," said the boy and Gunticus made a sort of grunt in reply. He took the snowshoes off his moccasined feet and thrust them, tails down, into a snowbank beside the door. They entered the crowded, steaming room together.

Gravely the Indian laid a penny on the bar and asked for hot cider. With the mug carefully held in both hands he retired to a corner and squatted there to enjoy his drink.

Dan took his usual place in the chimney nook where he could listen to the talk. The ruddy-faced farmer boys had a good butt for their jokes that evening—a soft-soap peddler who had arrived at supper time and asked for a night's lodging. He was a greasy-looking little man from one of the coast towns. On his one-horse sled he hauled two half-hogsheads of the strong grayish-yellow soap he had made at home from butchers' grease and lye, and sold his product to such improvident housewives as had no soap-kettles of their own.

A husky pod-auger man looked the peddler over and turned to one of his companions with a wink. " 'Pears to me," he remarked, "if I was sellin' somethin' along the road, I'd try to advertise my wares."

"That's right," returned the other with gravity. "Ye mean soap, fer instance?"

"Yeah. Seems like I'd sell more if folks thought I wa'n't scairt to use my own goods."

"Waal, if this feller's a walkin' example o' what his soap'll do, I certain' don't figger to buy none"—and so on, to the great amusement of the crowd.

The stage pulled in after a while and when the passengers had gone to their rooms upstairs, the pod-auger men prepared to bed themselves down. Instead of leaving, as he usually did, Gunticus spread his tattered blanket on the floor. Dan, on the point of starting for the barn, saw Skilly Bassett come over toward the old man's bed-place.

"Can't have ye in here," the landlord scolded. "Customers says they can't sleep with Injuns 'round. Don't like the smell. If ye ain't got no other place to lie, go on out to the barn."

Gunticus rose slowly and wrapped his blanket around him. Still dignified in spite of the teamsters' guffaws, he left the house behind Dan. Somewhat to the boy's distress he saw the old man pick up his snowshoes and follow him toward the stable. He wasn't exactly afraid of anything the Indian might do, but the idea of sleeping with an unwashed savage made him uneasy.

Inside, in the warm, breathing dark, he could hear Gunticus pushing aside the loose hay and stretching himself on the bare planks of the barn floor.

As they lay there, a few yards apart in the stillness, Dan was moved by a sudden impulse of friendliness. "Gunticus," he said, and the Indian made a noise as if he had rolled over to face him.

"Gunticus," Dan asked, "how do you make snowshoes?"

"Me makum easy," the old man answered proudly. "You want me makum for you, huh?"

He paused as if considering. "One moon me bringum tavern," he went on. "First ketchum deer, makum rawhide. Ketchum birch-tree 'longside river, makum frame."

"Honest?" said Dan. "Would you really make a pair for me? That'd sure be fine! I'd like to go 'round on top o' the snow, same as you do."

A few moments later he spoke again. "Gunticus, what's become of all the other Injuns that used to be 'round here?"

The old redskin shifted his position to sit erect. "My

people all gone," he said. "One time many wigwams, many braves. One time my people hunt, fight, fish from here to big water. Sickness come. Many go to happy hunting ground. Only Gunticus left. No more good to hunt. Mebbe killum one—two deer. Mebbe bear. Sellum fish. Sellum basket. Can't work. Can't steal. No good." He belched soberly and relapsed into silence.

Pitying him, Dan lay thoughtful for a while, then fell asleep. When he woke up at dawn the old Indian was gone.

. . .

As the weeks drew on toward Christmas, the stream of sleds on the road set strongly westward again. Many of the pod-auger men were on their way home now, with lighter loads of store-bought goods. They boasted of their purchases around the fire at night. Kitchen utensils, patented churns and farm tools, china silk and cotton print goods for the womenfolks to make into dresses. Combs and brushes, ornaments and ribbons and cheap jewelry for Christmas presents.

Dan, himself, felt the urge of giving that went with the season. He was rich now, for Skilly had paid him two months' wages. He went down to Henderson's general store, at the village cross-roads, and selected several articles with painstaking care. For Silas Penny he bought a polished iron belt-buckle, and for Silas' wife a comb made of some dark, gleaming wood. His gift to Ethan Hayes was a big, three-bladed jack-knife. And after some hesitation he blushingly purchased a string of blue glass beads for Molly.

The buckle and comb he wrapped in heavy paper and string and sent off by the post to Bellows Falls. In the barn he found a safe niche behind a beam where he hid the other gifts to wait for the arrival of the holiday.

Three days before Christmas the wind backed into the east, and leaden clouds forecast the coming of more snow. It began to fall early in the morning—hard, small crystals that stung Dan's face and whirled into miniature drifts along the fences. Travelers came in numb and half-blinded, with a frosty rime clinging to their eyebrows.

When the east-bound stage stopped to change horses, the driver had to be helped down from the box. His clothes were white with ice and his muscles were stiff from exposure.

"Only got one passenger," he said, when he could make his lips move. "Ye'll have to haul him out, I reckon. He's sick an' kind o' helpless. Told me when we stopped at Dublin he wanted to git ahead as fur's Deptford an' rest there."

Tim Garrity opened the sled-curtains and gave a hand

to the passenger within. After a moment a man in a huge, enveloping brown greatcoat and a fur cap climbed feebly out. He was tall but stooped and his feet

moved uncertainly as if he were very tired. He wore dark spectacles and a muffler high about his face but Dan could see that his cheeks looked gaunt and pale. With one gloved hand he carried a black leather case, and there was a small hair trunk which Dan shouldered, following the new arrival into the tavern room.

The man leaned on the bar for support and addressed Skilly Bassett. "Could I find lodging here for a few days?" he asked. "I am Dr. Barlow, a physician of Albany, in New York State. It seems I set out too soon after a serious illness and am not as strong as I thought." He paused to cough weakly, then went on. "All that's needed is rest, warmth and good food, such as I am told you provide."

Skilly hesitated, looking at him somewhat askance, and the doctor quickly drew a purse from the pocket of his coat. "Whatever your charges may be," he smiled, "I assure you I shall be glad to pay them." He opened the purse and laid a five-dollar note on the bar. "There's something in advance," he concluded pleasantly.

The landlord's attitude changed at once. "Put the gentleman's trunk in the sou'west bedroom, Danny," he cried, rubbing his hands. "An', Doctor, afore ye go upstairs, what about a drop o' the special brandy to take the chill out o' yer bones?"

As Dr. Barlow kept to his room and had his meals brought upstairs, he dropped out of Dan's thoughts completely in the next day or two. The boy was wholly occupied with the coming of Christmas and the preparations that attended it.

In the kitchen Mrs. Bassett and the maids flew around, as Tim expressed it, "like chickens with their heads cut off." The landlady was busy with an extra big baking of pies and getting ready two plump geese for the roasting spit. Dan did his chores, ran errands and tried to keep out from under foot. When the morning work was done, the day before Christmas, he took an

ax from the wood-shed and went up into the back pasture in search of a balsam fir. Finding a small one that was both bushy and symmetrical he cut it and bore it proudly to the tavern.

As the green branches came through the door Skilly Bassett burst into a cackling storm of protest. "What in all tarnation d'ye call this?" he yelped. "Mean to clutter up my keepin'-room with evergreens an' sech folderols? Take it out, durn ye!"

Dan stood his ground stoutly. "I thought it'd look pretty, an' remind the customers o' Christmas," he answered. "Look, Mr. Bassett—I'll stick it up here in the sawdust box. 'Twon't take up any room, hardly!"

Before the landlord could catch his breath for another tirade, a pod-auger man by the bar spoke up briskly. "I'm a poor hand to talk," he said. "Ain't goin' to make it home in time to celebrate, myself, this year. But blamed if that tree don't look good to me! Makes me want another glass o' flip 'fore I go."

Skilly said no more, and the tree stayed in the sawdust box. Grinning to himself, Dan stole out to the barn and got his precious packages. He was hoping to leave the yard unobserved, deliver his gifts, and be back before anyone missed him. But he had barely passed the pump when he heard his name called from the kitchen door.

It was Sue, the hired girl. "Missus says ye're to fetch an armful o' short wood an' take it up to the doctor's room," she told him.

Groaning inwardly, he put his two little bundles in a safe spot and loaded his arms with wood. There was a small fireplace in the southwest room, he now recalled, and the sick man had said something about needing to keep warm.

He climbed the stairs and went along the chilly hallway toward the doctor's door. It was nearly closed but unlatched. With both arms full he had no way to knock, so he pushed the door open with his foot and started in.

Seated in an armchair by the hearth, the thin, bowed man made a sudden movement. The black case had been open across his knees, and at the sound of Dan's entrance he swiftly closed it. The boy hesitated, then murmured a good-morning and crossed the room to the wood-box. Without venturing another look in the doctor's direction, he came out, closing the door behind him. But as he went down the stairs his heart was thumping queerly. In the brief instant while the lid of the case was closing, he had caught a glimpse of its contents. And he could have sworn it was not pill-bottles he had seen, but a pistol!

TEN

ALL the way to the Hayes farm, Dan puzzled over that half-hidden object in the doctor's bag. Perhaps he had been wrong. For all he knew there might be surgical instruments with brass-bound butts and trigger-guards. And, he asked himself, even if he had been right, was there anything strange in a man's carrying a pistol in his baggage when making a long journey? In the end he laughed at his own imaginings and went up the snowy lane whistling.

Mrs. Hayes greeted him hospitably at the kitchen door. Ethan, she said, had gone with his father to the wood-lot. Wouldn't Dan come in and wait? No, he told her, he had just come to leave something for Christmas, and he handed her the package. At the good lady's insistence he accepted a couple of her famous hickory-nut cookies and went on his way toward the village.

His feet moved more slowly as he approached the comfortable white house of the Crandalls, on the main street. Shamefaced, he looked up and down the road to

make sure no other boys were observing him. At the last
minute his confidence failed him. He laid the little
parcel on the door-sill, knocked loudly, and fled. From
behind a big box bush in the yard he peeped out in time

to see Molly open the door. She looked in all directions,
finally spied the package, and took it into the house
with her. Dan was whistling again as he started back to
the tavern.

A holiday spirit pervaded the Fox and Stars that
evening. The roads were good and sleigh-bells were
jingling up and down the pike from supper-time till

after midnight. Neighbors by the dozen dropped in for a Yuletide mug of flip or a glass of the hot rum punch that Skilly had prepared in his big old china punch-bowl.

Dan went to bed later than usual, but long after he had fallen asleep he was roused by a sound of clear voices singing. Somewhere down the hill a hayrack-load of young people serenaded the village with Christmas carols.

When the boy woke again, dawn was lightening the dusty windows. He sprang up eagerly, remembering the day. Then, as he pulled on his worn old clothes some of the thrill went out of him. There wasn't much for a stable-boy to expect of Christmas. It wouldn't be the same as when his mother was alive. But after all, he'd had the fun of giving, which was the best fun of all. He thought pleasurably of Ethan, opening the parcel and finding the knife. And that other package, to Bellows Falls—he hoped the mail had gone through safely.

Tim was late that morning. Dan had been at work for half an hour before he appeared, stifling a great yawn. "A Merry Christmas to ye, lad," he mumbled. "An' be thankful ye wasn't dhrinkin' Skilly's punch last night!"

They finished the early chores, washed, and went in to breakfast. The holiday spirit had evidently touched the two hired girls. They giggled archly and Kate tried to pin a spray of mistletoe in Sue's hair. But with the return of Maria Bassett to the kitchen they scurried back to their tasks like frightened mice.

"Come, come!" the landlady addressed the stable-hands. "Git to eatin', can't ye? Even if 'tis Christmas, we got work to do."

Dan pulled out his chair to sit down at the table. "Why—" he gasped—"for goodness' sakes!" On the chair seat were several paper parcels and the top one was tied up in narrow red ribbon. He saw his name written on it. With shaking hands he began to undo the packages.

The first one he opened was from Molly Crandall and it held a red wool muffler. As he held it up, the girls tittered excitedly.

"Knitted it herself, she did!" cried Sue. "Ain't it handsome?"

"It sure is," he said and felt his face reddening. Hastily he laid the gift down and turned his attention to the other bundles. There were two linsey-woolsey shirts that had come from Silas Penny by post. "They got here three days ago," Mrs. Bassett told him, "but I figgered 'twas a Christmas present, so I kep' it fer today."

From the Hayes family he received a high-crowned

cap with a shiny visor and ear-flaps. And in the last and largest package was a pair of new cowhide boots. There was no mark to show where they had come from, but instinctively he looked up at the inn-keeper's wife. She

was very busy, stirring cake batter in a big mixing-bowl.

"Try 'em on," she said, testily. "That trav'lin' cobbler makes mistakes sometimes."

Dan kicked off a worn-out boot and pulled on one of the new pair. "Perfect!" he exclaimed. "Just big enough to let my feet grow next summer. But how'd you know the size?"

"Land sakes, that's easy!" the woman replied, still stirring vigorously. "Don't ye recollect, when the shoe-maker was by here, last month, I had ye take off yer boots to git that rip mended? He measured 'em then, an' had 'em finished next day. That there leather's from

Uncle Enoch Estes' bull. Oughta be tougher'n all git out!"

Dan couldn't tell whether she heard his words of thanks or not—so furiously had she attacked the batter. But he had a warm feeling of gratitude toward the strange, grim woman. With a full heart, he started on his breakfast.

Tim had disappeared. Now he came back to the table with a sheepish look on his face. "Here," he said. "I clean forgot till me eye fell on the presents there. I've a bit of a gift fer ye, meself."

He tossed on the table a finger ring of bright iron, bent out of a horseshoe nail. "Put it on fer luck!" he grinned.

. . . .

That afternoon Dan put on his new cap, muffler and boots and walked down the hill to the village. Somewhat to his relief he found the Crandalls had gone somewhere on a visit. The house was locked. But at the Hayes farm the family was at home and he was given a wholehearted welcome. Ethan took him up to his room in the attic at once, to show him his Christmas presents. Such an array of gifts Dan had never seen. There seemed to be dozens of them—mostly useful, but all desirable. Ethan passed them over quickly, in haste to get to his pride and joy—a long-barreled squirrel rifle which his father had given him.

The two boys took it out behind the barn for target practice and fired several rounds before the early dusk made it too dark to see. Then they went in to pop corn over the coals in the kitchen. With a big panful of the flaky white kernels, salted and buttered, and a basket of ruddy winter apples, they spent as pleasant an evening as Dan could remember.

He got back to the inn before nine and was waiting in the big main room for the stage to arrive, when Maria Bassett called him. "More wood wanted upstairs in the doctor's room," she said. "Skip lively now, 'fore the poor gentleman's fire goes out!"

Dan knocked at the door this time, before he lifted the latch.

"Come in," said Dr. Barlow pleasantly, and the boy carried a big armful of wood to the box beside the fireplace. He was about to go out again when the doctor spoke.

"Sit down, lad," he smiled. "Have a sip of the hot cider. I get lonesome for a word with somebody, up here by myself."

He was reclining in an easy chair, his long legs thrust out toward the fire. A flannel lounging robe enveloped him, and he had on a tasseled night-cap. The dark spectacles were still on his nose.

"Christmas today, eh?" he remarked genially, holding his steaming glass in long, thin fingers. "Well, what's the news in the village?"

Dan, stiff and somewhat uncomfortable on the chair opposite him, replied that he hadn't heard of any.

Dr. Barlow laughed. "No news is good news, so they say. You did have some happenings of moment here a few weeks ago, I've heard."

In spite of the idle tone of the doctor's words, Dan felt a tenseness, as if he were being watched closely from behind those spectacles.

"I s'pose you mean the folks freezin' to death?" he answered uneasily. "Yes, that was kind o' bad."

Dr. Barlow sat perfectly still in his chair. "Tell me about it," he said after a brief pause.

The boy recounted the events following the blizzard, without going into great detail.

"Hm!" The doctor cleared his throat. "Too bad! And the child? What was done with it?"

"Mrs. Crandall, down in the village—she's takin' care o' Dolores."

"Dolores." Dr. Barlow repeated the name softly, as if musing over it. "Pretty name. And they've no idea who these people were?"

"Not till they get word back from Boston or Baltimore. The squire expects to hear soon, I guess."

"Ah, yes—the squire!" said Barlow with a silent, un-expected chuckle. "Well, lad—thanks for your gossip. And try to keep that wood-box filled. Good-night."

The stage was in the yard when Dan got downstairs and he was too busy for the next half hour to give much thought to the conversation he had just had. It came back to him as he was drowsing off to sleep.

"A queer bird—the doctor," he yawned to himself. "Pleasant enough, though. And he seemed real interested in hearin' about the baby. Must be a kind-hearted sort of feller."

.   .   .

The boy exchanged no more than a word or two of greeting with Dr. Barlow for several days. Then, one evening, he came into the keeping-room and found him ensconced on a settle by the fire.

"Ah, there, youngster," he smiled. "I've been feeling better, and decided to come down here for company. You might fetch me another glass from the bar, if Mr. Bassett'll be kind enough to mix it. A smart boy you've got here, Mr. Bassett."

"Hm—yeah! Too smart fer his britches!" mumbled the landlord, who was in one of his usual sour humors. "Take the glass, Dan, an' mind ye don't spill it."

Dr. Barlow smacked his lips over the toddy and seemed to be looking about for a topic of conversation.

His glance moved along the wall to the paper which still remained tacked up there.

"I see they've posted a reward for that highwayman," he remarked. "What's his name—Captain Hairtrigger. Desperate sort of fellow, by all accounts."

"Aye," said Skilly. "Desp'rate enough, but we chased him out o' these parts with his tail 'tween his legs."

Noah Winslow, the jovial miller, who ground wheat at the lower falls, chuckled to himself and cleared his throat.

"I heard a tale or two 'bout the cap'n when I was over to Concord last week," he said. "There was a peddler from Boston at the tavern where I was stayin'. Said folks in Massachusetts figgered there wa'n't a jail built strong enough to hold this feller. He's busted out o' two of 'em already, an' next time they aim to shoot him dead.

"From stories I hear he must be a 'cute devil though. One time they say he stayed a month or so at a tavern in Lexin'ton. Run up a big board bill an' the landlord begun to be anxious about his pay. He got paid, all right —in hard money, too—an' this was the way of it. Seems this inn-keeper owned a fine bay hoss, with two white forefeet an' a white star in his forehead. 'Twas kep' in a pasture, a mile or so from the tavern. One night when

Hairtrigger—he had another name then—got sick o' bein' pestered fer his board, he strolled out there an' stole the hoss. Ridin' over to the next county he sold it fer a pretty tidy sum, then hung around an' stole it again the next night. The day after, he come ridin' back to the inn. He'd cropped the hoss's mane, thinned out his tail, an' dyed the star an' the white feet bay color.

" 'Landlord,' he says, 'I b'lieve I picked up a bargain fer ye. This here hoss'd certainly go pretty with that white-footed bay o' yourn. They're like as twin brothers fer size an' gait. I 'most hate to part with him myself, only they'd make sech a dandy pair. I'll let ye have him fer a hundred dollars.'

"Well, the inn-keeper jumped at it. Soon as he handed over the money, the hoss-thief paid his bill, ordered a round o' drinks fer the house an' walked off. 'Twan't till the white hairs begun to show through the dye, a few days later, that the landlord went rushin' up to his pasture an' found out what had happened."

Dr. Barlow leaned back on the settle and his sides shook with laughter. Everyone in the room joined in the roar of merriment except Skilly. His mirth was only half-hearted. He never could appreciate a joke when it was on a tavern-keeper.

When the chuckles subsided, Noah Winslow's voice began to rumble again, ponderous as his own mill-stones.

"Folks over Concord-way seem to think this Hairtrigger's tied up with the Stingers," he remarked.

There was a moment's silence. Then the doctor spoke. "Who," he asked, "might they be?"

"The Stingers?" replied big Ben Tucker. "Thought everybody'd heard o' them—even over in 'York State. They're a band o' cut-throats an' thieves that work all the way from Pennsylvania to the Canada line. We ain't seen much of 'em 'round here, I'm glad to say. Mostly they rob freighters an' pod-auger men—hide the stuff in barns an' sech. Then at night they haul it on to the next gang that's in cahoots with 'em, an' so on till it's fur enough away to sell."

"Tch, tch!" The doctor made a clucking sound with his tongue. "A distressing state of affairs! What are the authorities about, that they allow it?"

"Authorities do their best," said Ben with a grin. "They've caught a few—enough to know there's a lot more of 'em loose. But they're a tough crew to tangle with."

"Well, gentlemen," smiled the doctor, "I've had an enjoyable evening, but if my health is to continue improving, I'd best get to bed. Good-night to you all."

He eased his long, thin body erect and limped to the door at the foot of the stairs. They heard him go slowly upward, a step at a time.

"Seems like a pleasant sort o' feller," Noah Winslow nodded after him. "Eddicated, too. I'll bet he's a real smart doctor."

ELEVEN

WHEN Dan went out after supper the next evening, there was a surprise awaiting him in the yard. Six big horses stood there steaming in the snow, and a burly driver was just climbing off his loaded sled. No second glance was needed to tell the boy it was his old friend, Silas Penny.

"Silas!" cried Dan joyfully. "I'm sure glad to see you. Thought you'd laid up fer the winter. What brings you on the road again?"

The freighter grinned. "Figgered this sleddin' was too good to miss," he said. "There was a good pay load to be hauled to Nashua, so I hitched up an' started, Christmas day. I'm on my way back now."

They put up the team and went into the tavern room, where Silas was greeted by all his acquaintances.

"How's the road 'twixt here an' Keene?" Skilly Bassett asked him.

"Fine!" the teamster answered. "Slicker'n grease. I could've pulled most of it with jest the wheelers."

"That's good," said the taverner. "Reckon I got to go over there tomorrer. I rented a hoss an' sleigh to a feller trav'lin' through last week, an' the rig hain't come back yet."

Penny took a long drink of cider and looked at the landlord with a twinkle in his eye. "Be sort o' tough to go off when business is so good, won't it?" he asked innocently.

"Yes, durn it!" Skilly replied with a scowl. "I'll lose money by it."

"Hm!" said the freighter. "I jest got an idee. This boy here's good with hosses. Why don't ye let him ride over with me an' fetch the rig home?"

Bassett brightened visibly. "That'll be a real help," he answered.

"The hoss is stabled at Richardson's tavern. That where you put up?"

"Sure—there or the Phoenix," Penny nodded. He winked at Dan. "Better git to bed early, son," he said. "We'll be startin' by four o'clock."

So it came about that Dan was tramping along beside the sled in the star-sprinkled dark, next morning. It was so cold that the breath froze in hoar-frost on the horses' muzzles. At first the boy felt the chill in spite of the warm thickness of his wool clothing. Then, as he hurried to keep pace with the fast-stepping team, the blood quickened in his arteries and the cold bothered him no longer.

Silas Penny strode along in silence at first. Then, when his vocal cords were thawed out, he gave the boy such news as there was from Vermont. The Christmas package had arrived in plenty of time, he reported. And to prove it, he opened up his bearskin great-coat and displayed the belt-buckle Dan had sent. "Ye couldn't ha' pleased my wife more if that comb had been the crown jewels of Rooshy!" he added. "She was hopin' I'd see ye on this trip, an' sent her regards. Said she wanted me to ask special how them shirts fit ye."

After sunrise the air began to grow warmer, and they were able to ride the sled without discomfort. Before noon they reached the relay-house in Dublin, where they stopped an hour to rest the horses and eat dinner.

The landlord was a bustling little Irishman with a wen on the end of his nose. As he thrust their plates of steaming corned beef and cabbage before them he rubbed this deformity violently and gave a great sneeze. "The cold got in me bones last night," he explained. "Faith an' we had grand excitement here. I was out till all hours."

"What happened?" asked Silas, his mouth already filled with food.

"Bedad, 'twas robbers was in it!" cried the little man.

"A pod-auger sled from beyant the river come through here afther sundown. Not three hours later the pore driver crawled back to the dooryard. He was beat somethin' terrible, his head cut open, an' all he owned in the worrld stole from him. He told us three big fellers in rough clothes an' masks over their faces shtopped him half-way to Marlboro. Whin he put up a argyment, wan of 'em bashed his head wid a cart-stake. An' be the time he woke up, his sled an' horrses was gone. There was half a dozen of us in the bar an' we set out wid guns to ketch the blackguards. But divil a sign o' them could we find. The snow in the road was packed so hard ye couldn't tell wan track from another, an' we saw no place where they might ha' turned off."

Penny had paused in his eating, the loaded knife half-way to his mouth. He frowned now, and his glance moved toward Dan. "I don't like that," he said. "Sounds like the Stingers to me. Is the driver still here?"

"Aye, that he is, pore feller. An' how he's to git back home I couldn't tell ye."

"I'll talk to him," said the big teamster, resuming his dinner.

When the two had finished eating they were led into a back room where the victim of the robbers sat disconsolate in a chair by the fire. He was young—under twenty, Dan thought—and in answer to Penny's questions he said he came from up Rutland-way. His father had sent him to Boston with a fine load of butter and frozen beef. Now he was on his way back. The cloth and the money he had gotten in trade were stolen, along with a team of good, sound horses and the new sled. He was heartbroken, as Dan could well understand. And the pain of his injured head under its bloody bandage must have deepened his despair.

"Now listen, young feller," said Silas kindly. "I'm goin' through to Bellers Falls, where I live, an' I'll carry ye that fur. From there on I reckon we'll find some way to give ye a lift. You ready to travel now?"

The young farmer had had his dinner and was grateful for the invitation. They made him as comfortable as they could amongst the freight on the sled. And by twelve o'clock they were back on the road again.

Dan and the teamster hiked along beside the rumps of the roan wheelers. For a time Silas said nothing. Then abruptly he asked the boy a question. "How 'bout drivin' back alone tomorrer? Ain't scairt, be ye?"

Dan laughed. "Of the Stingers, you mean? Not a bit."

"That's good," the freighter nodded. "It ain't really dangerous in daylight, anyhow. Most o' these robberies I've heard about have been after dark."

They plodded on, with the great white dome of Monadnock lifting against the sun to their left. When they had made some five miles along the road, their passenger called to Penny to stop. "I think this is the place," he said. "They come out from under that tree, ahead."

He climbed stiffly down and led the way to a trampled spot in the snow by the roadside. "Guess that's my blood," he said, sheepishly pointing to a red stain. "I must ha' laid there five minutes 'fore I come to."

Dan had gone on a few yards farther, toward the tree. "Look at this," he called. "Here's some tracks comin' from over back o' the wall."

In the jumble of foot-prints they made out three separate tracks. They were too blurred to be worth anything as clues, but judging from their size all three must have been made by big men.

"Yeah—they were big an' no mistake," the young pod-auger man nodded ruefully. "All more'n six foot, they looked. Gosh! I was foolish, I guess, to try to fight 'em—but I couldn't help it, thinkin' o' Paw an' what he'd say—"

"Shucks!" said Silas comfortingly. "I know jest how ye felt. An' I don't believe yer paw'll hold it agin' ye."

Before sunset they passed through Marlboro, and an hour later the lights of Keene twinkled below them in the valley of the Ashuelot River. The freighter clucked cheerily to his horses and the leaders pricked up their ears, stepping faster at the prospect of grain and warm stalls.

They trotted down the last hill with a jingle of harness bells and pulled up the wide main street to Richardson's tavern. As soon as the team was stabled and supper eaten, Silas introduced Dan to the proprietor of the inn. Mr. Richardson was an elderly man, with a red, humorous face and a bush of white chin whiskers. His eyes twinkled when he heard where the boy was employed.

"By thunder!" he exclaimed. "Don't tell me ye got that much meat on yer bones workin' fer Skilly Bassett!"

Dan flushed. "Well," he said, "I work for Mr. Bassett, but it's his wife that cooks the meals."

At that the inn-keeper let out a great bellow of laughter and slapped his thigh. "I'll have to tell Skilly that 'un, next time I see him," he chuckled.

Dan was amazed to hear that there were half a dozen other hotels in the town, all doing a rushing business. Keene was a stagecoach center, with roads radiating from it to many points of the compass. The bulk of the farm-sled traffic from Vermont also passed that way, and it was no uncommon thing for two or three hundred travelers to sleep at the Keene taverns in a single night.

They kept later hours, too, Dan found, than at a little country inn like the Fox and Stars. It was past ten o'clock before the pod-auger drivers, the coachmen and passengers, the peddlers and bag-men had begun to settle down for sleep. The boy made his bed between Silas and the young Vermonter and finally drowsed off.

He was wakened by candle-light at five in the morning. Silas was already up, washed and ready for breakfast. "Ye'd best make an early start," he told Dan. "It's clouded up dark, an' feels like snow."

They ate in the big dining-room—a good breakfast, Dan thought, but nothing to compare with "Black Maria's" meals. By six he had paid for his lodging, helped Silas harness the sled-team and bidden his big friend farewell. Then he went back to the stable to get Skilly Bassett's horse and sleigh. It was not the fast mare, Lady, he was to drive home, but a big-boned, hard-mouthed sorrel of uncertain age, which Skilly sometimes rented as a livery horse. Mustard was his name.

Dan found him hard to handle. Several days in the stall had made him "fat an' sassy," as the hostlers put it. He bucked and reared but finally submitted to being bridled and backed between the sleigh shafts. There was a heavy blanket on the seat, and a mangy old bearskin robe. Dan wrapped them snugly about his legs, gathered the reins and took the whip out of the socket. "All right," he called to the stable-man. "Open the door an' stand from under!"

As the big barn door swung wide, the sorrel made a mighty plunge and jerked the sleigh out into the yard at full gallop. Dan, sawing at the bits, managed to make the turn into the street on one runner. Fortunately the thoroughfare was wide and there were few teams out at that hour of the morning. He held the horse down as best he could till they were out on the Deptford pike. Then he gave him a smart cut with the whip. "Go ahead, now!" he said. "You're so durn frisky—let's see you go tearin' up this hill!"

The sorrel soon quieted down as the grade steepened, and by the time they were out of the valley he was acting docile enough. Warm under the robes, Dan enjoyed the brisk pace. He had never driven so far alone, and it made him feel responsible and important. Twenty-two miles, Silas had told him it was, from Keene to Deptford. With the fine sleighing he ought to get there in three or four hours, even allowing for the many hills that would have to be climbed at a walk.

Just as he was making these calculations, a big flake of snow settled softly on the bridge of his nose. Mustard tossed his head and snorted. The air was full of feathery gray now, and even in the east, where dawn ought to be breaking, the sky was leaden and dark. Dan pulled the red muffler up around his chin and huddled down deeper into the blanket. Ahead of him, the horse's sorrel back had turned completely white in a few seconds. He had never seen snow fall faster.

For the next half hour the boy strained his eyes into the silent tumble of flakes and tried to guide the horse. Then he realized it was hopeless. Twice he had nearly tipped the sleigh over by pulling too far to the side of the road. Finally he gave Mustard his head. The big horse was no longer eager, but he pushed along willingly enough into the blinding curtain of white.

The wind was rising. Dan could feel it whipping his cheeks and hear its roar in the thrashing branches of the pines. It was growing colder, too, and the big, soft flakes of snow had broken into small, hurrying particles that would make drifts all too quickly.

It made the boy feel helpless to sit there in the sleigh and let the dumb brute in the shafts bear all the burden of getting them safely home. Angrily he climbed out and walked beside the curving dash, holding on to the reins. But it was a pointless thing to do, for he could barely see as far as the horse's head and his feet stumbled continually in the eddying drifts. At last he got back in and was thankful to wrap up in the robes once more.

After what seemed a long time, Mustard whinnied and quickened his pace. Dan saw a house looming up to the right, only a few yards away. Then he realized they were in a village—Marlboro it must be. He pulled up at a hitching post in front of a little store, threw a blanket over the horse and went in.

There was a big old wall clock ticking above the counter, and it said ten minutes to eight. Not much more than an hour and a half for the five miles he had traveled. And the storm wasn't likely to get worse. Encouraged, he warmed his hands by the stove a moment.

"How far do you call it to Dublin?" he asked the storekeeper.

"Oh, round about ten mile," was the casual answer. "Sort o' mean trav'lin' though, ain't it? Most o' the sled drivers has put up at the tavern an' won't stir out today."

"I guess I'll make it," said Dan, trying to sound like an old hand at the business. "Got a good fresh horse an' a light sleigh."

A moment later he had taken the blanket off Mustard and was heading eastward again, into the storm. As the blurred outlines of the houses slipped behind, the thought of the lonely miles ahead began to daunt him. He felt himself a very small speck in the limitless fury of wind and snow. For a moment he was tempted to turn and go back. His hands wavered on the reins. Then, as the white curtain lifted a few seconds, he saw the horse's head still high—the big shoulders boring steadily forward—the stubborn drive of the thigh muscles—and he was ashamed. Mustard wasn't quitting, and he wouldn't, either.

For the next six hours he saw no living thing except the good nag between the shafts. Once he thought he heard a dog howling faintly through the scream of the wind. It might have been a wolf—there were still wolves in those hills, old-timers said—and the boy shivered at the sound. Then the smell of wood-smoke borne by on a gust reassured him. He was passing a farmhouse.

There was no way to measure distance. Dan thought he must have been in the sleigh a long time, for his legs were numb, and the drifts along the road were getting deeper. The horse's progress was slowed to a laborious walk now. Sometimes he floundered in snow above his belly and advanced only by short forward plunges. It was colder, too. With terrible clearness, Dan remembered the frozen bodies that had been carried to the inn after the big blizzard. He shook himself angrily and shouted encouragement to the struggling sorrel. Surely it couldn't be much farther to Dublin—unless the horse had missed the road.

The sleigh tilted forward over the brow of a hill and Mustard moved down at a weary trot. They were descending into a valley where the force of the wind was

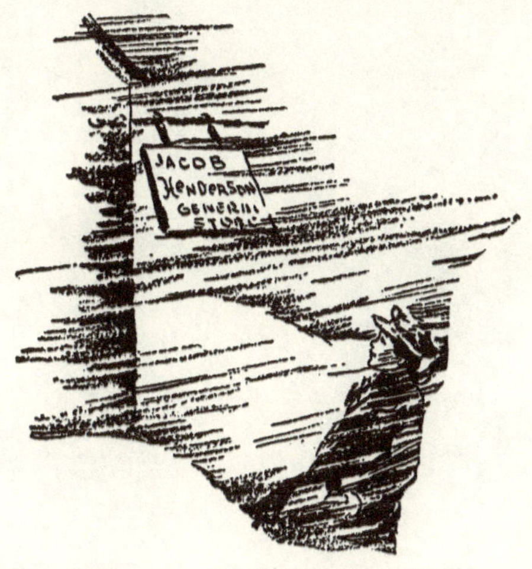

broken and the snow was less heavily drifted. Shadowy shapes that looked like houses stood close to their path. Dan plucked up heart. They must be in Dublin village at last, and if he could find the relay-house he would take shelter there.

Anxiously he strained his eyes into the whirl of flakes. Ahead there was a creaking noise—a sign swinging in the wind. He hauled sharply on the sorrel's hard mouth and the sleigh moved nearer the sound. There it was, close above him. He stared at the swaying board and rubbed the snow out of his eyes. To his amazement the sign read—"JACOB HENDERSON, General Store." He was at Deptford Four Corners, barely a quarter of a mile from home!

TWELVE

THAT last climb up the hill through the drifts was the hardest part of the whole journey. Dan got out, to lighten the sleigh, and wallowed along in its wake for the final hundred yards. It was beginning to grow dark when they reached the tavern at last, and candle-light made a feeble glow in the windows. As soon as the good sorrel was rubbed down and fed, the boy went in through the sheds to the kitchen.

Skilly Bassett was standing by the stove talking to his wife. He turned and stared at Dan as if he saw a ghost.

"G-great jumpin' Jehosaphat!" he sputtered. "Mean to say ye druv through from Keene in this? Don't ye know ye might ha' lost a good hoss an' rig, let alone yerself. Why in tarnation didn't ye put up at Marlboro —or Dublin? I thought ye had more sense—"

"That's enough, Skilly!" the landlady snapped. "Can't ye see the youngster's tuckered out? Pretty spunky of him, I'd call it. How long since you et, Dan?"

"Breakfast," the boy mumbled sheepishly. "I meant to stop at Dublin—honest. But I never saw a sign of it.

The snow was so thick I must ha' come right through the place an' didn't know it was there. Mustard kep' plowin' along, an'—well—here we are!"

"Set down at that table," commanded Mrs. Bassett. "Supper's most ready anyway an' it won't take me two shakes to rustle ye up some vittles! Skilly, ye ought to be proud o' the boy. 'Tain't many that'd have that much gumption."

Before morning the snow had stopped falling. Out in the clear, pink dawn with his shovel, it was hard for Dan to realize that he had been in any danger, twelve hours earlier. The wind had gone down, and the glittering crests of the drifts looked fresh and innocent. He fell to work with a will and had the path to the pump half dug before Tim yelled a good-morning from the barn door.

"Begob," cried the hostler, "I thought to find ould Mustard a broken-winded wreck, what wid the hammerin' he took yestiddy. But here he is as spry as a kitten! Listen at him whinnyin' afther his breakfast!"

"Best snow-hoss in the township!" replied Dan stoutly. "Guess you heard how he come through Dublin so fast I never even got a look at it!"

.   .   .

The morning chores were hardly done when the plows came whooping up the hill, and by mid-afternoon traffic was moving as usual. Even the down stage got through from Keene, arriving at supper-time, nearly four hours late.

Just as Dan finished stabling the horses, a dark figure appeared silently in the fringe of lantern-light. The boy looked up, startled, and saw a dingy blanket and an old slouched hat.

"Why, Gunticus!" he exclaimed. "You sure scared me, sneakin' up like that!"

"How!" the old Indian greeted him. "One moon go by. Me bringum snowshoe. Here."

He opened his blanket and held forth a pair of new frames, filled with laced rawhide. Dan took them wonderingly, and examined the skillful workmanship with awe. The straight-grained wood of a split birch had been steamed and bent symmetrically into bows, then lashed in place with strong leg-sinews of a deer. The buckskin thongs that made the filling were cunningly woven and knotted so that they would neither stretch nor slip.

"Gosh!" Dan breathed. "They're the best ones I ever saw. I want to pay you for 'em, Gunticus."

He was reaching into his trousers pocket when the Indian held up his hand and gave a grunt of displeasure. "No wantum money," he said. "You good boy. Me bringum present."

"Oh," replied Dan, a little taken aback. "Thank you, Gunticus! But it must have been a long job makin' 'em. I'd like to give *you* a present, too." He stood thinking a minute, then remembered his old jacket, hanging on a peg in a dark corner of the barn. It had three tarnished brass buttons on it. Quickly he went to find it, cut off the buttons with his knife and returned with them in his hand.

"Look," he said. "Here's your present," and he dropped the buttons in the Indian's palm. Gunticus stared at them and a smile wrinkled his old face. "Fine present," he beamed. "Me put 'em on hat."

He took off the battered old headgear and solemnly debated where he would sew on the buttons to give the grandest effect. Dan, meanwhile, was tying the snowshoe straps over his boot-toes. When they were firmly on his feet he clattered awkwardly out into the snow. Once in their natural element, the shoes ceased to be encumbrances. Light and strong, they bore him up on top of the drifts. At first he walked clumsily, tripping himself and knocking the frames together. But in a moment or two the trick of it came to him. Out on the smooth snow by the yard-fence he tried a few experimental running steps and found, to his delight, that he was able to jog along without a tumble.

"Listen, Gunticus!" he panted, coming back to the

A DARK FIGURE APPEARED SILENTLY
IN THE LANTERN LIGHT

barn. "You got to let me buy you a mug o' cider, anyhow. Let's go in now."

The Indian seemed to welcome the suggestion. He followed Dan into the keeping-room and solemnly accepted the hot cider that Skilly poured for him. Then, squatting in a corner, he proceeded to sip it as slowly as possible. His leathery face was impassive as always, but Dan knew he was happy.

For a week there was fair, cold weather. The roads were packed hard by steady travel, and farm-sleds crowded the inn-yard once more. Dan found plenty to do, but whenever he could get an hour to himself he was out on his snowshoes. The snow was still deep in the fields. He could trot across to Ethan Hayes' house in half the time it took to go around by the road, and he made the trip often. The redhead was overcome with envy when he first saw Dan coming over the drifts. After trying the snowshoes himself, he set out immediately to make a pair.

"Look," he said, enthusiastically, "I've got the hide o' the red calf we butchered last fall. An' birches are the easiest things there are to find. I'm goin' to start right now!"

But it was a good deal more difficult than he imagined. He broke the first set of bows in the bending, after hours spent in whittling them out. And after a few attempts to cut rawhide into straight, even thongs he abandoned the idea.

"Spring'll be comin' soon, anyway," he told Dan one day, a week or two later. "Mebbe next year I can git on the right side of ol' Gunticus an' he'll make a pair fer me."

It was a fine afternoon toward the end of January when the Crandalls' sleigh pulled into the yard and Dan saw Molly and her mother, with little Dolores, go into the tavern. A few minutes later one of the kitchen girls called him, to carry wood to the doctor's room. He had already taken up his daily armful and the request surprised him. It hadn't been especially cold that morning, and he couldn't understand how the supply had been used up. Nevertheless, he loaded his arms with short sticks and climbed the stairs.

Dr. Barlow could hardly be called an invalid any longer. From the hearty meals he ate and the quantity of spirits he consumed, anyone would judge him a well man. However, he had stayed on at the inn, remarking jovially that he found the clear mountain air good for his constitution. If Skilly Bassett worried about his board bill, he had made no complaint in Dan's hearing.

Reaching the door, the boy knocked and was told to enter.

"A good afternoon, lad," the doctor greeted him. "I

thought I might be reading late tonight, and 'twould be handy to have some extra fuel for the fire. By the way, didn't I just see some people arrive below?"

"Yes," said Dan.

"A little child, I believe. Could that, perchance, be the orphaned baby you told me of—the one whose mother—er—"

"That's who it is," Dan nodded. "Little Dolores, with the Crandalls. Payin' a call on Mrs. Bassett, I reckon."

"Ah, yes," said the doctor. He rose and put on his blue coat. "I may go down," he remarked lightly. "The case interested me, and I should like to see the child."

As Dan came down the stairs Molly spied him from the parlor and called to him. Bashfully he entered the room and greeted Mrs. Crandall, cap in hand. Dolores' eyes, huge and dark in her pale little face, turned toward him and she smiled. "Boy make bells wing!" she said.

"Hear that?" laughed Molly. "She hasn't forgotten you, Dan. And neither have I, though I haven't seen you since Christmas. Look—I've got the beads on! They were a lovely present!"

Fumbling for words the boy was trying to thank her for the red muffler, when Dr. Barlow appeared in the doorway. In his fine blue coat, flowered waistcoat and tight gray breeches that strapped under his shining boots, he looked quite handsome, Dan thought. Much younger, too, than the boy had realized. He still wore the dark spectacles, and a black silk skull cap hid most of his hair. For the first time, it occurred to Dan to wonder what color the doctor's hair was. Queerly enough he had never seen him without a hat or a cap on.

"I beg your pardon, Mrs. Bassett," Barlow smiled. "Hope I don't intrude. Just heard the little one's voice and thought I'd drop in. I'm very fond of children, you know."

A bit flustered, the landlady proceeded with the introductions.

"I'm real glad to meet you, Doctor," Mrs. Crandall said, earnestly. "I've been worried some about Dolores. She's such a thin little thing, and she don't seem to gain. I've wanted to take her to old Dr. Reynolds, but he's been so poorly of late—"

"Yes, yes, Mrs. Crandall," the doctor broke in. "Of course—of course. I'll be glad to look at the little girl. Come here, my dear. Let me see your tongue."

Dolores, always shy with strangers, stared at the man in the dark glasses and began to cry. He bent down and peered into her open mouth before she turned her head away.

"Hm," he said. "Tongue coated. Doesn't gain properly. I'd better take her pulse."

He pulled out his big gold watch, took the child's wrist between his fingers, and counted in silence. At the end of a minute he stood erect and slipped the watch back into his waistcoat pocket. His mouth looked grave and thoughtful.

"Her condition," he said, "is not really serious. However, it should be watched. I have some medicines in my case and will let you have something to give her. A moment, please."

With that he bowed himself out of the room and they heard him climb the stairs. The two women beamed at each other. "It's certainly a relief to hear him say that," Mrs. Crandall smiled. "Such a kindly way he has with children, too, and he's such a gentleman!"

Molly Crandall, standing at the back of the room with Dan, stifled a snort. "I don't like him—gentleman or not," she whispered in the boy's ear. "Do you?"

Dan shook his head. He could not tell her about his own doubts. They were too vague—hardly more than a sense of something in the doctor's personality that didn't ring true.

Almost at once the man was back, folding some pills into a sheet of note paper as he entered the parlor. "One of these every two hours in the day-time," he told Mrs. Crandall, "and keep her warmly wrapped at night. I expect to be here a few days longer, and if you don't mind I may call at your house to see the child again."

"Oh, if you could, Dr. Barlow, that'd be just fine!" the good lady replied. "I haven't got my purse with me, but you let me know what the bill is and I'll have the money for you."

"We don't need to mention that," laughed the doctor, deprecatingly. "Really, this wasn't a professional call, you know. Glad to be of some service."

As the conversation went on, Molly pulled at Dan's sleeve. "Come—let's get out of here," she whispered. "He makes me sick!"

Tiptoeing in her wake, Dan followed into the kitchen. "Say," he offered, "want to see my new snow-shoes? Ol' Gunticus made 'em for me. I can run on 'em an' everything!"

Out in the yard he demonstrated his skill, and let her try the snowshoes on, herself. She was long-legged and strong—a regular tomboy, as Ethan often said. In five minutes she was walking as if she had been born with snowshoes on her feet.

"Gee!" said Dan admiringly. "You got onto it quicker'n I did. You know you're all right, fer a girl!"

"For a girl!" she stormed, kicking off the snowshoes. "I can do anything you can do, Dan Drew! That is—'most anything." Her angry eyes twinkled suddenly into a smile. "I don't know's I'd want to drive through from

Keene in a blizzard," she finished.

"Aw, shucks," said Dan, embarrassed. "That wasn't much. The hoss did it—not me. But listen, Molly—I didn't mean—"

She laughed at him. "I know," she said, "you men-folks never mean to belittle us women. Here comes Ma and the baby. I'll have to run—good-by!"

Dan watched them go and wondered if he should have confided to Molly the story of the pistol he thought he had seen in the doctor's medicine case. No, he decided, there was no use in worrying the Crandalls with any such fanciful idea as that. All they wanted was to have Dolores well and happy, and if Dr. Barlow's pills accomplished it, why fret about anything that might seem strange in his actions? Besides, from the way he had spoken in the inn parlor, he would be leaving soon. Gone and forgotten.

But the boy couldn't help thinking, as he went back to the stable, that it might not be a bad plan to keep an eye on the doctor. He'd like to know, just for curiosity, how the man looked without those spectacles.

THIRTEEN

IT was snowing lightly the next afternoon, when the east-bound stage changed horses. Tim Garrity, who claimed to have uncanny powers in the matter of forecasting weather, announced that the snow was just a flurry. "Ye'll be seein' stars be the time ye're ready fer bed," he told Dan. "The big storms is over fer the winter."

As the boy led out the fresh team of leaders, he saw Amos Crandall coming out of the tavern door with Dr. Barlow.

"I won't be away long," the Deptford man was saying. "Just travelin' over to Concord on business. Probably back in three days. It'll be a relief to me though to know you're keepin' watch over the baby."

He shook hands with the doctor heartily and followed the rest of the passengers into the big covered sled.

That evening Dan was sitting by the fire in the keeping-room when Dr. Barlow came downstairs. He had on his greatcoat and fur cap, and was wearing boots. The black medicine case was in his hand. For a moment or two he talked to Skilly Bassett in a low voice. The inn-keeper seemed reluctant about something but he finally nodded and beckoned to Dan.

"Doctor wants to pay a visit at Crandalls'," he told the boy. "The sorrel's rented out to that feller from Nashua. Ain't a hoss in the barn 'cept Lady, so I guess he'll have to take her. Hitch her up to the light cutter an' bring her 'round to the door."

The pretty little mare had not been out of her stall for three days, but Dan had no trouble with her. If she was restless she took it out in playfully nudging his arm with her soft nose while he was putting on the bridle. The silver shaft bells made a musical accompaniment to her swift trot, as he drove her out to the tavern entrance.

Dr. Barlow was in a jovial mood when he came out. He had been sampling some of the special brandy, Dan thought, for his laugh was loud, and his usually pale face looked flushed in the candle-light.

"Well, good-by, boy," he said as he took the reins. "Good-night I should have said. Ha—ha! Look for me back in an hour or two."

He clucked to the mare and sped out of sight down the turnpike hill. The snow, Dan saw, had almost ceased falling. He stared after the vanishing sleigh a moment, then walked slowly back to the tavern, his feeling of dislike for the doctor stronger than ever.

That evening seemed to drag interminably. Dan dozed by the fire and waited for the arrival of the night stage. It came in half an hour late, with Nate Gilman

on the box. The fat driver was swearing roundly because one of his wheelers had cast a shoe. "Ain't a smith on the whole run from Boston can drive a nail solid!" he raged. "Tomorrer, Dan, you take the hoss down to Ben Tucker an' git him shod right. He's one man that knows his business!"

The boy helped Tim Garrity stable the horses and returned to the keeping-room. It was after ten by the old clock over the bar. Past his bedtime and still no sign of the doctor.

Skilly Bassett looked up from polishing flip-glasses and scowled at the clock. "Dunno what's keepin' him so late," he said testily, "—'less mebbe the young 'un is real sick. Anyhow, ye'd best wait up fer him, an' make sure the mare is dry an' bedded well before ye turn in."

The boy went back to the settle and tried to keep awake by watching the shifting pattern of flames that licked the great back-log in the fireplace. He was just stifling a great yawn when the door burst open and a scared-looking boy stumbled in. He was panting so hard he could not speak for several seconds and there was a general uproar as the men in the room gathered about him. A couple of pod-auger drivers, who had been asleep in their blankets, sat up, startled, and shouted that there was a fire. At last Skilly succeeded in shaking an intelligible reply out of the youngster.

"That doctor feller—" gasped the boy—"he was at Crandalls'. When Mis' Crandall was in the other room he grabbed the baby up an' run out. Molly chased after him, hollerin', an' he fired a pistol at her—hit her in the arm. Two men started after him afoot, but he druv the sleigh out the north road a-flyin'. They're gittin' hosses an' follerin' him now."

"Thunderation!" groaned Skilly. "Why did I ever let him take the mare? They'll never ketch her! How long ago was it he started?"

"Not more'n half an hour," the boy answered. "I was 'crost the road at Henderson's an' Jake sent me up here a-runnin', soon's he heard of it."

"An' we ain't got a hoss left in the barn!" the innkeeper moaned.

All this time, Dan had been standing open-mouthed, staring at the village lad. The news had rocked him back on his heels. Little Dolores—stolen! Nothing he had imagined about the doctor had been as bad as that. The pistol he could believe, but that it should have been fired at Molly Crandall—that she was wounded—he gritted his teeth and strode toward the other boy.

"Are you tellin' the truth?" he asked in a low voice. "Listen—how bad is Molly hurt?"

"I—I dunno!" mumbled the village youngster. "I didn't see her. All I know's what I heard."

Dan turned suddenly toward Nate Gilman, the stage driver. "Those leaders o' yours looked pretty fresh," he said, "an' we need hosses. They'll work under saddle, won't they?"

"Sure—sure," nodded the plump coachman. "Take 'em, an' welcome—jest so I don't have to ride 'em."

"All right, Mr. Bassett," said Dan. "I'll saddle 'em— an' you'd better call Tim!"

He didn't wait for an answer but sped toward the stable as fast as he could run. The coach-horses had finished their grain and were drowsing in their stalls. They acted surprised and disgusted when he flung saddles on their backs and jerked the cinches tight. A moment later he was booting his mount across the yard, pulling the other horse after him by the bridle-rein.

The inn-door stood open. He saw Skilly Bassett, his bald head bare, waving an excited arm to someone inside, and then Tim Garrity appeared, buttoning his jacket. The Irishman was still stumbling and bleary-eyed with sleep.

"Here!" yelled the inn-keeper after him. "Ye'd better go armed!" Rushing out into the cold starlight he thrust a horse-pistol into the hostler's mittened hand. "It's loaded an' primed," he said impatiently. "Come—git up an' ride, can't ye? That durn doctor's got my mare and he owes me a month's board besides!"

Dan didn't wait for Tim to swing into the saddle. He kicked his boot heel into the big horse's side and went out of the yard at a lumbering gallop. He kept to the deeper snow at the roadside to save his mount from slipping, and went thundering across the bridge at the foot of the hill with Garrity close behind. As they came into the village they saw a little knot of people standing in front of the Crandall house.

Dan pulled up his steed in a flurry of snow. "How's Molly?" he panted—and then, "Which way'd they go?"

One of the old men answered in a squeaky voice. "Molly ain't hurt bad—jest a flesh wound in the arm. Ever'body's gone to chase the doctor feller—up the Hancock road."

They wheeled their horses and dashed off, swinging north at the crossroads. There was no moon, but the sky was clear and the snow reflected enough starlight for them to see their way. As they rode abreast up the beaten track, Tim pulled closer. "Divil a glimpse we'll get o' the doctor tonight!" he grumbled. "Don't they know how that mare can trot? She'll be in the next county be now!"

"Sure," Dan answered shortly. "But we got to try. Think o' that baby!"

"Right y'are," the hostler agreed. "The dirrty spalpeen! If on'y I had a dacint horse under me!"

They must have covered five miles when Dan heard voices and the clink of horseshoes ahead. In another moment they could see a cluster of dark shapes moving toward them. A horse whinnied, and Tim's nag tried to answer but found itself too short of breath.

"Whoa, boy," said Dan and pulled his mount down to a walk. "Who's this comin'? Must be the Deptford men."

Sure enough, as they drew nearer they could recognize Ben Tucker's broad shoulders hunched above the leading horse. In a moment the blacksmith hailed them. "Who's there?" he asked.

"Tim Garrity an' Dan Drew from the tavern," the hostler replied. "Where's yer prisoner?"

"Durned if I know," growled Tucker. "We rode 'most to Hancock Village, an' not a soul up there had seen him. Must ha' turned off on one o' the side roads. There's sleigh tracks on all of 'em. Ain't a chance in the world o' trailin' him tonight."

Disappointed, Dan turned his horse and rode homeward with the crowd of villagers. They made a formidable-looking, if motley, array, with their horse-pistols, Queen's-arm muskets and squirrel rifles. The troop passed several small roads, leading off to east and west, and the boy lagged behind, studying the jumble of sled and sleigh tracks that led up them. In the dark it was hard to distinguish fresh marks, for only a sprinkling of snow had fallen. Once, however, he thought he saw prints that had been made since afternoon. If he had carried a candle and flint and steel he might have made sure. As it was he climbed down from his horse and felt along the clean runner-marks with his bare fingers. The posse had ridden on, too far ahead for him to call. Reluctantly, he mounted again and trotted after them.

Climbing the hill to the inn, Dan told the hostler what he had seen, but his companion was too sleepy to give his words much attention.

"That's nothin'," Garrity yawned. "Sleighs is as thick as flies in harvest-time. Which road was it?"

"It runs up to the east'ard just beyond that stretch o' woods," the boy replied. "Only a couple o' miles from the village, I should say."

Tim shook his head impatiently. "He wouldn't be shtoppin' that close," he said. "Besides, the road don't go nowhere. I ain't never been on it, but it just leads to the Nixon place. Belikes 'twas one o' their rigs made the tracks."

.   .   .

In the morning, Dan was hard to rouse. He had lain awake till long after midnight, cudgeling his brains for an answer to the mystery of the doctor's disappearance. Tim's arguments had left him unconvinced. He wanted to know more about those sleigh tracks before he gave up. Sleepily he performed the morning chores, then washed and went in to breakfast.

The kitchen wenches were in a dither of excitement. A wild rumor had started in the village to the effect that Dr. Barlow was an escaped lunatic and a cannibal. What he might already have done with the baby, Dolores, was too horrible to be imagined.

While Dan had too much common sense to believe the story, he could muster very little appetite for buckwheat cakes and sausage. Leaving his plate full he went into the keeping-room.

Skilly Bassett's face was a picture of dejection. "It beats all," he was telling a group of early arrivals, "how I could be took in by sech a scalawag. A gentleman he was, by the look of him, but I should ha' made him pay cash from the start. We opened that hair trunk o' his this mornin', an' what do ye think was in it? Bricks! Nothin' else, except a few pieces o' soiled linen an' his old coat. That's all I got to show fer forty dollars' wuth o' food an' liquor an' a mare that was wuth two hunderd of any man's money!"

Out of breath, he paused and dolefully regarded an empty cider mug on the bar. Dan screwed up his courage and stepped closer.

"Mr. Bassett," he said in a low voice, "I think I saw the mare's tracks last night."

"What's that?" The inn-keeper was suddenly all attention.

"On a side road, a couple o' miles north. It was too dark to be certain, but if you'll give me a little time off I'd like to cut across there on my snowshoes—"

"Oh, so that's it?" the landlord replied bitterly. "Allus lookin' fer a chance to git out o' work!"

"You know that's not it," Dan told him, trying to be patient. "I'll work overtime if you want, to make up.

But I'm as anxious as you are to get Lady back—an' the little girl—"

"Ye're right, I s'pose," Skilly nodded gloomily. "It don't sound like much of a chance to me, but go ahead. If ye do find anything git back here spry. They aim to hold a meetin' here at the tavern this mornin'."

The air was damp and the sky cloudy when Dan slipped his feet into the snowshoe thongs. He knew it might start snowing again at any minute, and it behooved him to hurry. Instead of going around by the road he cut straight through the pasture, in the direction he and Ethan had taken on their gunning expedition. He wished the other boy could be with him now.

Dan's months of living in Deptford had given him a better sense of the town's geography. He had a fair mental picture of the way that little side road must take, winding up to the Nixon place, but to make sure, he headed for the clearing itself. In half an hour he saw open ground through the trees ahead.

This time the boy was careful not to show himself. He stopped in the edge of the woods to reconnoiter. There was the roughly built barn, and the house with a wisp of smoke drifting downward from its chimney. Neither dogs nor humans were in sight. Skirting the clearing to the left, he came in a few moments to a narrow woods road leading in from the west.

Dan's heart was pounding hard as he crouched, staring at the tracks, there in the snow. Straight, clean marks of sleigh runners. And between them the prints of dainty hooves, headed toward the clearing. There were other horse-tracks—bigger ones—pointing in the

opposite direction. But the east-bound prints were those of a light road-horse, and the boy had a breathless sense of certainty that he had seen that right front shoe nailed on.

There came a rustling noise behind him and he sprang up in fear. Suppose they caught him here, unarmed! The sound, he discovered, was nothing more than a wind stirring the dead leaves on a scrub oak, but he lost no time in moving back into the woods.

One thing more he must know, and that was whether Tim had been right when he said the road stopped at Nixons'. He followed his own tracks in a wide circuit of the clearing and went on to the eastward, with flakes of snow blowing in his face. It was coming down in white flurries by the time he had reached the farther side, beyond the buildings. No sign of a road appeared. He was on the point of turning back when he saw a freshly broken alder-branch a few yards ahead. Beside it ran a narrow track, hardly wider than a foot-path, and in the trail, half-blurred already by the new snow, were a horse's hoof-prints. No sleigh had passed here, he knew. And the tracks had been made by a big horse, going at a gallop.

Dan waited to see no more. He struck off through the woods, making such speed as he could, and arrived at the tavern some time before noon. The barn was full of saddled horses, and a dozen empty sleighs and pungs stood about the yard. As soon as the boy got his snow-shoes off he made his way into the crowded keeping-room.

A big man in home-spun clothes was shouting above the confusion of voices. He had a ruddy, reckless face, fringed with a bush of red whiskers, and he was gesticulating with a half empty glass of rum. Dan caught a few of his words. ". . . if we don't ketch this rascal

an' string him up . . . safety of our wives an' chil-
dern . . ."

Somebody snickered, close to the boy's shoulder and
he turned to see Tim Garrity. "The likes o' *his* wife
oughta be safe enough!" murmured the Irishman.

"Why?" asked Dan. "Who is he?"

"Newt Nixon—him that's married to Big Liz!" came
the chuckling reply.

The boy stared. "Newt Nixon!" he gasped. "Why,
he's the man—say—I got to talk to Skilly right away!"

FOURTEEN

IT took Dan a moment or two to wriggle his way through the packed throng in front of the bar. When he did reach Skilly Bassett's side the red-bearded man had subsided and two or three others were clamoring to be heard. Above their shouting rose the high, squeaky voice of Asa Pease, the constable. The boy caught a glimpse of him, standing on the settle by the fireplace, waving his short, fat arms frantically for order.

"Ye got to quiet down now, or we won't git nothin' done!" he yelled. "Shet up, every one of ye!"

In the comparative quiet that followed, Dan was able to catch the landlord's attention. "Mr. Bassett," he said, low and urgently, "can you come with me a minute?"

The inn-keeper squeezed out from behind the little bar and followed the boy into the hallway. "What is it?" he asked. "Ye found anything?"

"Yes," said Dan. "Those tracks go up the road to Nixons' an' stop there. An' they were made by the mare—I'm sure as shootin'!"

"Ye don't say! Nixons'? Why, that don't seem possible. He's here—makin' more noise'n anybody."

"I know," the boy replied. "But there's no doubt
about those tracks. If only it wasn't snowin', I could
take Ben Tucker over there. He made the shoes an' he'd
be able to tell."

Skilly's brows were puckered in thought. "Guess
there's jest one thing to do," he said. "That's to tell Asa
Pease—if I kin git a word with him. You stay here,
Danny, an' I'll see 'f I kin bring him out."

Dan fidgeted there in the chilly hall for several minutes. Then the door of the keeping-room opened and
he saw Skilly Bassett with the constable in tow.

"So this is the boy," Pease remarked. "I remember
him. Well, young feller, what's this ye've got to report?"

Dan repeated his story and watched an incredulous
smile spread on the officer's fat face.

"No, no," he shook his head when the boy had finished. "Nixons may be rough sort o' folks but I reckon
they mean well. Newt pays his taxes reg'lar. Here—I'll
see what he has to say."

And before Dan could make any objection he had
darted back into the crowded room. When he reappeared, the big bulk of the red-whiskered backwoodsman loomed behind him.

"This boy, here," the constable began at once, "thinks he saw tracks made by the doctor's sleigh a-leadin' up to your clearin'. What about it, Newt?"

Nixon gave a silent chuckle and his pale blue eyes roved over Dan speculatively. "Guess likely he did see some tracks," he grinned. "I druv in there last night with that little roan trotter o' mine. I'd been down to Henderson's store fer provisions. But after that I was home all evenin', an' I kin tell ye positive no doctor come up our way. Don't blame the boy fer his mistake, though. If we had a few more as smart as him, things would be a heap better 'round here."

Dan's jaw dropped. The frank and open way Nixon spoke took all the wind out of his sails. Asa Pease laughed and patted his shoulder. "There now," he said, "I thought we'd git to the bottom of it, lad. But don't ye feel upset. We all make blunders once in a while. Now let's git back to business."

While the discussion of plans went forward in the tavern room, Dan took his way slowly to the barn. He felt foolish and ashamed, but at the same time he was angry. The man's explanation had been too glib. And there were still things he would like to know. Who, for instance, had ridden off so fast on that trail through the woods? It was too late now to ask any more questions, he realized. Sore and humiliated, he turned to the job of catching up with his morning's work.

At dinner-time Tim Garrity told him what had happened at the indignation meeting. "Whin they got done hollerin' an' ravin'," he said, "ol' Pease come out wid some good idees. He wants to form a troop o' citizens—a vigilance committee, he calls it—ready to ride the minute the worrd is passed. Ivery man is to be well-armed an' a good shot. I was wan o' the first wans picked," he concluded modestly.

"Fine," said Dan. "But is that goin' to catch the doctor, or bring back the baby?"

"Aisy now," the Irishman replied. "We ain't fergittin' that parrt of it. 'Tis this very afthernoon they're sindin' out search parties in different directions. Pease is cap'n o' wan troop, Ben Tucker of another, an' Newt Nixon the third—"

"Who?" Dan choked on a mouthful of boiled potato.

"The big, red, hairy feller—Nixon," said Tim. "He's handy wid a gun an' strong on talk."

The boy pushed his plate away. Somehow he didn't feel hungry after that news. "Well," he said bitterly, "I don't reckon they'll find much."

He kept himself busy that afternoon polishing harness. It was the kind of job he could do in an empty box-stall at the back of the barn where nobody came. Nevertheless, Ethan Hayes found him there when school was out. The farm boy was too full of excitement to notice his friend's gloomy mood. He came bursting in, shouting Dan's name and hauled him out of his hiding-place.

"Listen!" he exclaimed. "They've picked me fer the vigilance committee, an' Paw says I kin jine up! Gee, Dan—think o' that! I got my new rifle oiled up an' I'm goin' to practice shootin' with the men down to the village! Jest wait till that ol' doctor comes 'round here again—I'll draw a bead on him like this an'—*bang!*"

"That'll be fine—if he comes," Dan nodded soberly.

"Well, him or any other des'prit character," said Ethan, a little taken aback by the stable-boy's coolness. "Say, ain't you anxious to ketch Barlow an' git Dolores back?"

"You bet I am!" Dan replied. "But I don't believe he'll be caught by just waitin' fer him."

"Oh, we're layin' plans to go after him," Ethan exclaimed. "An' what I wanted to tell ye was that mebbe I kin git you in the troop, too. Newt Nixon says every able-bodied man oughta jine up—"

"Yeh," said Dan, "I know—'fer the safety of our wives an' children.' I thought you didn't hold much truck with those Nixons."

"I guess I was wrong about Newt," Ethan answered in some embarrassment. "He's takin' a big part in gittin' recruits fer the committee. An' they say he kin fight like all git out!"

"All right," said Dan wearily. "Maybe I made a mistake. I'll be glad to go in, if there's any way I can help."

Overjoyed at his friend's decision, the farm boy rushed off to the committee headquarters at the blacksmith shop, and by noon of the next day Dan found himself officially enrolled as one of the town's defenders. For a weapon he had Ethan's old smooth-bore musket—the one he had carried on their partridge hunt. And Skilly Bassett, fired by the general fervor that was sweeping the village, allowed him two hours off every afternoon to drill with the troop.

Earnestly, if somewhat clumsily, the men and boys marched and counter-marched in the snow. Just what good these military evolutions would do in capturing Dr. Barlow, Dan never found out. But the target practice that followed was something he understood and enjoyed. The vigilance committee had raised money for several kegs of black powder, which was passed out in liberal amounts to all who had guns. And the banging and shouting that went up from the target range was enough to wake the dead in the church-yard.

Dan learned quickly. While his old flint-lock was far less accurate than Ethan's rifle at long distances, he was soon able to hold his own with any of the marksmen when it came to shooting at closer range.

Twice he went out with mounted details, ordered to search lonely farms and tracts of woodland on the outer edges of the township. Hardly a day passed without some rumor sending the horsemen galloping off on such an errand. For miles up and down the Contoocook, terrified women barred their doors at night and hid their children in the garret. Baby-stealing was something unheard-of in the valley. It had brought hysterical fear to scores of peaceful homesteads. Uncle Mose Morrison, driving a sled-load of fire-wood down from Half Moon Pond, stopped at the tavern to gossip a little.

"Puts me in mind of Injun times!" he told Skilly Bassett. "Hain't seed the womenfolks so skeert in fifty year! Why—durned if my wife'd let me come to town this mornin' without I got a neighbor in to set with her!"

Expertly he aimed a golden stream of tobacco juice at the middle of the sawdust box, and took a long pull at his mug of cider. " 'Course," he resumed, "nobody up our way has seed hide nor hair o' the doctor feller. But t'other mornin', 'bout daybreak, a man on a big black hoss went tearin' past the house, headed north. Marthy seed him an' made me git down my musket. Might ha' thought she was 'feared o' bein' scalped! I dunno who 'twas, but most likely one o' these town milishy boys.

They don't seem to hev nothin' to do but go gallopin' 'round the country."

Dan, coming in with an armful of wood for the great fireplace, heard the old man's last speech. He dumped the sticks in the wood-box and stood staring into the flames, thinking. A man on a big black horse, riding north at daybreak. When Uncle Mose went out to his sled the boy followed him.

"Did you get a good look at that man—the one on the black horse?" he asked.

"Nope," the grizzled backwoodsman replied. "Not me. But Marthy did. I'm satisfied 'twan't the doctor. This 'un was tall an' straight. No spectacles. Wore boots an' a brown greatcoat an' fur cap, pulled down 'round the ears. Wal, youngster, come up to Half Moon an' pay us a visit some time."

Dan thanked the old-timer and watched him guide his lumbering oxen out of the yard. That description of the dawn rider had stirred his imagination. He knew of no big black saddle horse anywhere in Deptford, and he thought he had seen every mount used by the troop. Could Captain Hairtrigger have come back to the valley again? With his brow puckered in a frown, he went to get his gun for the daily drill.

There seemed to be more excitement than usual in the broad, level field by the river, as Dan came down the hill. In addition to the thirty-odd men and boys who were accustomed to gather there, he saw a score or more of women and older men standing about in little groups.

"Hey, Dan!" Ethan Hayes yelled to him. "There's goin' to be a shootin' match! Uncle Amos Crandall's offered a dollar—hard money—fer the best shot in the troop!"

They were already pacing off the range. It was to be fifty yards, Dan was glad to see. He might have a chance at that distance. The target was a round, wooden half-peck measure, about nine inches in diameter, tied to the top of a post. Laughing and boasting, the members of the "milishy," as the old people all called them, loaded their guns and made ready to try their skill. They were to shoot in turn for three rounds, Dan was told. There were concentric circles drawn in chalk on the target, numbered from one to five. And the bull's-eye itself, which counted ten, was no bigger than an old-fashioned shilling piece.

All the shots had to be made standing, and without a rest. Ethan and Dan stood together, near the end of the line, and watched one after another of their comrades take his aim and fire. There were a good many misses, but every once in a while some lad from back in the woods would send a slug surprisingly close to the center spot.

Ethan's turn came, and he lifted the new rifle proudly. There was a shout from the scorers after he fired. "It's a ten!" someone yelled. "Square in the middle!"

"Great!" Dan grinned, slapping his friend on the back. "That's the first bull's-eye anybody's made!"

"Go ahead an' lay one in there yerself!" Ethan laughed and pushed him up to the line.

Dan knew his gun and its shortcomings. There was no wind to allow for, but some twist in the old musket's barrel always carried the bullet to the left a few inches. He drew his bead, not on the small white center of the target, but on its right-hand edge. Then gently he squeezed the trigger.

Through the smoke he saw the markers running in to check his shot. "Four!" one of them called. " 'Bout an inch too fur to the right."

On the second round one of the other men hit the

ten-spot, but his first shot had counted only one. When Ethan placed a bullet in the five-ring, he was still leading by four points.

Dan faced the target again. He allowed less this time, holding just to the right of the middle, and got a five, his slug flying a hair's-breadth too far to the left.

"Good goin'!" Ethan cried. "You're third now. I guess we'll show 'em we ain't too young to shoot!"

A breeze sprang up just as the third round started. It was blowing from the north, gently, but enough to affect the shooting. There were fewer hits on this round. The man with the score of eleven over-estimated the wind's strength and missed the target completely. Ethan, full of confidence, took a quick aim and fired. It was a hit but farther out than his first two shots—right on the line between the three and the two circles.

"Call it a two," the boy told the scorers. "That makes seventeen, don't it? Reckon that ought to be enough."

Dan was trying to gauge the wind. It was, he thought, lighter than most of the marksmen had realized. He need not allow more than an inch or so. And the wind was against the natural pull of the gun—just about equal to it. He took two or three deep, slow breaths and lifted the musket. The sight came to rest squarely on the tiny disc of the bull's-eye. At the steady pressure of his finger the gun roared.

There was no call from the markers. They were grouped around the battered half-peck, peering at it with close attention.

"What's the matter?" some of the competitors yelled impatiently. "Git out o' the way an' score it a miss!"

A sudden stir was seen among the men by the target. "We found it!" one of them shouted. "Square in the spot! Come so close on top of Ethan's, we couldn't see it at fust!"

The freckled farm boy gasped, then gave a whoop. "By golly, Danny!" he cried. "That wins it! You got a nineteen!" There was no disappointment in his face. He was genuinely glad of his friend's success.

The rest of the men shot out their string and the scores were tallied. Then Amos Crandall was walking toward the markers. He took a paper that one of them handed him and came back to stand in front of the troop. It was the first time Dan had seen him since his return, and he was shocked by the change in the man. His kindly face looked gray and drawn, his eyes tired.

"You fellers have been practicin' hard," he said. "I can see it's done you some good. That was fine shootin'. Don't know as my old militia company could have made as good a showin' back in 1812. I promised to give a dollar to the winner, an' I'm glad to do it. Some o' you might come up with that doctor that took our little girl"—he stopped a moment to steady his voice—"an' when you do I want to know you're able to shoot straight. Guess that's all I had to say—except that here's

the dollar. Looks like it was won fair by—let's see— Dan'l Drew. He shot a bull's-eye, a five an' a four for nineteen points. You're a credit to the town, Dan, an' I'm proud to give it to you."

When the shining silver piece was laid in his hand, the boy could find no words to reply. He mumbled an embarrassed "thank you," and tried to hide himself again in the crowd of amateur soldiers. But he was too slow to get away from Molly Crandall. Her arm still bandaged and in a sling under her coat, she darted through the hilarious group and found him.

"That was grand!" she said, her face aglow. "And I'm 'specially tickled to have you beat Ethan. He's bragged so loud about that rifle—"

"Here!" her cousin grinned. "I'd wash your face in snow fer that, if it wa'n't fer your havin' a little bullet scratch in the arm!"

Dan laughed. "Can't you quit fightin'—you two?" he asked. "Listen—there's the stage horn blowin', up beyond the village. I've got to hustle!"

And with a light heart he loped up the hill toward the tavern.

FIFTEEN

THE news of Dan's prowess as a marksman spread quickly through the township. When he passed the blacksmith shop next day, Ben Tucker left a hot horseshoe in the fire long enough to come out and congratulate him.

"Guess I was pretty lucky," the boy said. "I just figgered right on the wind when I made that last shot." He was showing his big friend the musket when his eye chanced to fall on the horse that was being shod. It was a small, neatly built roan in driving harness.

"Whose hoss is that?" Dan asked. "Don't remember seein' him before."

"Oh, that's Newt Nixon's trotter," the smith replied. "Beauty, ain't he? Newt druv in this noon an' left him while he went over to the drill ground."

Dan stepped closer, studying the roan's feet. The bare hooves were broader and rounder than the Lady mare's, he thought. "Where's the shoes you took off him?" he asked Ben, casually.

"Over there on the pile. Them two top ones is off his
front feet."

The boy picked one up and studied it. "Calks all worn
off?" he asked.

"Yeah, Newt said he was slippin'. Wanted him sharp-
shod."

Dan tossed the shoe back on the scrap pile, trying to
appear unconcerned. "Well, I got to step along to drill,"
he remarked.

But as he crossed the bridge he was seething with inward excitement. If he wanted proof that Nixon had
been lying, that day of the meeting at the inn, he had it
now. For the shoe-prints he had seen in the woods-road
had shown deep, new toe and heel calks such as he knew
the bay mare wore.

He looked in vain among the men on the field for
Nixon's heavy shoulders and red beard. Apparently the
backwoodsman had some other business on hand besides
drilling his shambling recruits that day. He did not show
up during the hour they spent marching and going
through the manual of arms. But when Dan started
back to the inn he saw that the roan horse was gone
from the smithy.

He wished, now, that he had taken Ethan into his
confidence. It would be a help to talk to somebody
about his discovery, but he was too certain Tim Garrity

or Skilly Bassett would scoff at anything he might say against Nixon. He went about the afternoon chores and kept his mouth shut.

That night, when the stage from the East came in, there was a stranger on the box beside Nate Gilman. Dan caught a glimpse of a brace of pistols in the fellow's belt, as he swung to the ground. The coachman flung the reins to Tim Garrity and climbed down after his companion. They stumped about for a moment to get the stiffness out of their legs, then went to the deep boot at the back of the sled. As Dan took the lead team toward the barn he saw the two men entering the inn behind the shivering passengers. Between them they carried a heavy-looking wooden chest, and each was shouldering a sack of mail.

Tim had stopped for a word with Gilman. Now he was whistling as he led in the wheelers. Dan could see that the Irishman was bursting with news, but in spite of his own curiosity he did not ask questions. At last Tim could keep it in no longer. "Bedad!" he said, " 'tis quare business is goin' on, whin Natey Gilman drives wid an arrmed man to guard him! 'Phwat's in the box?' sez I, an' they tells me 'important mail.' An' thim sweatin' to lug it! Must be turrible hefty letters in that mail!"

Dan finished bedding the stage team and went to the

keeping-room. The man with the pistols was snoring on the settle by the fire and Gilman was engaged in low-voiced conversation with the landlord.

"Here he is now," Skilly Bassett said. "Come here, Dan."

When the boy had joined them in the corner by the bar, the inn-keeper leaned closer. "Reckon ye seen the box Natey was carryin' in," he whispered. "Important mail from Boston, goin' through to Brattleboro. 'Course 'tain't likely anybody's goin' to bother the stage up this way—not with the vig'lance committee so active. Still, they don't want to take no chances. Nate brung a feller along from Nashua to set up front with him an' sort o' keep an eye on things. But he don't want to go on no further."

The fat coachman nodded. "So," he put in, "I jest asked Skilly if I could git the best shot in Dep'ford to ride the next stage. An' he tells me nobody kin shoot like you, youngster."

Dumbfounded, Dan looked from one to the other of them. "You—you mean it?" he asked. "You want me to go?"

"Sure," Gilman replied. "Ain't scairt, be ye?"

"No, o' course not," Dan assured him hastily. "I just thought maybe it was a joke you were playin' on me. I can shoot, all right, but I never had to shoot at a—

at a man."

Nate Gilman's fat paunch shook with laughter and he patted Dan's shoulder. " 'Tain't very likely ye'll have to," he said. "Load up yer gun an' be ready fer an early start. I aim to haul out by four, so's to git to Brattleboro 'fore dark. I'll leave ye off at Dublin an' ye kin git the down stage back this afternoon."

The boy walked back to the barn with a queer sense of importance bulging his chest. He had been picked for a man's job—a post of danger and responsibility. Whatever was in that box, locked in the tavern closet now, it must be something valuable. Money, probably. In any case it had to be guarded well. And Gilman had chosen him to do it!

By the feeble light of a pierced tin lantern he cleaned the old musket, rammed home the powder and ball and inserted a fresh flint in the hammer. Then he laid it carefully in the hay beside him, extinguished the candle and curled up in his blanket. For more than an hour he lay wide-eyed, too excited to sleep. When at last he did drowse off, it seemed as if he was wakened the next moment.

Tim Garrity stood over him, yawning in the lantern-light. "Roll yerself out, Danny," he growled. "Begob, 'tis a sinful hour to be gittin' up, but Natey's unaccountable anxious to make a starrt."

Dan sprang up and hurried into his clothes. Shivering, he helped feed the stage-horses, then ran to the tavern for his own breakfast. The kitchen-girls were sleepy and so were the three coach-passengers, gobbling a hasty meal in the dining-room. In a few minutes there came a blast from Gilman's cow-horn. Dan pushed back his chair and went out at once.

It was pitch-dark in the yard. Even the stars were hidden by heavy clouds. By the faint glow of light from the stable-door, the boy could see the stage dimly outlined against the snow, and Tim Garrity leading out the wheelers. He put the harness on the lead-team and helped with the hitching-up. Then, while the passengers bundled themselves inside and Tim and the coachman stowed the heavy box safely in the boot, he went to the stable for his musket. Making sure that he had a full powder-horn and pouch of bullets, he put fresh priming in the pan and hurried to join Nate Gilman on the box.

"Here," said the stout driver, cheerfully, "wrap this double blanket 'round yer legs. It's almighty cold, this time o' the mornin'."

The boy tucked the blanket under him and laid the musket carefully across his knees. Then, as Gilman cracked his whip, the snorting horses pulled the traces taut. The runners, frozen down in the night, worked loose and began to move forward, whining on the hard snow. And the confused jangle of the harness-bells settled into a mellow rhythm as the team struck its gait.

They crossed the bridge at the foot of the hill and passed the dark shapes of houses in the sleeping village. When they were out on the road beyond, Nate Gilman spoke again. "Cold gittin' in yer bones?" he asked.

Dan tried to keep his teeth from chattering. "No," he said, "I'll make out all right."

His companion, he realized, had fortified himself with a morning bracer. A pungent aura of Medford rum hung about him, and every few moments his head nodded forward drowsily. It was a good thing, Dan thought, that the road was packed smooth and the horses knew their way. He found it hard enough to keep awake, himself. The steady pace of the team, walking up the hills and trotting down them, brought a lulling sense of security. And in the cold and the dark, it was much easier to huddle under the blankets and let his mind wander than to concentrate on the twisting road ahead.

Once, toward the end of that first hour, he caught himself dreaming and jerked angrily erect. Not a cutter or a pod-auger sled was out as yet. The dim white alley between the close-crowding woods lay empty as far as his straining eyes could reach. And yet he fancied he had heard a sound—the snort of a horse, faint and at a distance.

They were climbing a little rise. Dan remembered the place from his earlier trip—a lonely stretch of road—no farms within a mile. It would, his roving imagination told him, be an ideal spot for a robbery. With the team slowed down and climbing at a walk, what an easy thing it would be to stop them! A chill of panic ran up his spine, but he mastered it and tried to laugh at his own fears. Common sense told him the chances were fifty to one against anything of the kind taking place. He resisted his impulse to rouse the dozing coachman and sat back instead with an air of nonchalance. Still, he would feel better when they were over that hill. Close to the top, now. Only a few seconds more and they would cross the ridge. He drew a deep breath and closed his eyes with relief. And in that instant the stillness of the night was shattered by a yell.

"Hold hard, there!" a rough voice roared. Before Dan's startled eyes three tall figures ran out from the brush on the right. One of them had seized the off leader's bridle-rein. The others were advancing toward the stage. Gilman woke with a sudden gasp and hauled back instinctively on the lines, making the horses rear and plunge. Hardly knowing what he did, Dan found himself standing up, the musket at his shoulder.

"Get back, you!" he shouted. "Stand away or I'll

shoot!"

He was aiming straight at the nearest of the three men.

"Let 'em have it!" croaked the driver, and with a pounding heart the boy pulled the trigger. A sickening, dull click answered the pressure of his finger. The gun had misfired!

One of the men laughed in a queer, husky voice that froze Dan's marrow. He was a great hulking fellow with a dark cloth covering the lower part of his face. As he made a lunge toward the driver's box, Dan swung the useless musket by the barrel, in a desperate effort to club his huge assailant down. Then the gun was snatched out of his grasp and flung aside into the snow. He felt a big hand tighten painfully on his arm. He was dragged down and given a stinging cuff on the ear that knocked him to the ground. Dizzy, his head ringing with the blow, he lay in the snow trying to gather his wits.

The robber who held the horses' heads shouted impatiently to his companions. "Git on with it! We ain't got all night!" And a moment later he saw the coachman and the three passengers lined up beside the road. One of the ruffians was covering them with a pistol while the other—the one Dan had tried to shoot—was pawing over the contents of the boot at the back of the sled.

"Here 'tis!" he heard that strange, husky voice chuckle. "Heavy enough, too!"

The big man swung the box to one broad shoulder and staggered up the road with it. "Hold 'em right here till I git back!" he growled to the others. "I'll bring the hosses."

There was a wait of perhaps five minutes. Dan, helpless and bitter in the knowledge that he had failed, tried to get up once and was warned by a gesture of the man with the pistol to stay where he lay. Finally the third robber reappeared over the crown of the hill, leading four horses. One had the chest tied on its back with ropes, and the rest were saddled.

For the first time, the man with the pistol spoke. He was nearly as tall but slighter in build than his companions, and his voice was cold and precise. At the sound of it an echo of memory woke in Dan's numbed brain.

"You will stay where you are," he said, "until we are

out of sight. If a man moves he will be killed."

Like the others', the man's face was masked, but Dan thought he could have told how that face would look. A second glance at the waiting horses made him certain. For even in the shadowy dimness before dawn he recognized the slim, powerful legs and proud head of the great black.

One by one, the three highwaymen swung into their saddles. For a moment they sat regarding the coach and its motionless crew, then wheeled their horses without a word and galloped out of sight over the hill-top.

The tense group beside the stage moved at last: "Go ketch a holt o' them leaders!" the coachman snapped sullenly at Dan. "They'll run away if ye don't step quick."

While the boy held the heads of the nervous team, Gilman hustled his passengers into the stage and investigated the boot. "All right," he called, at length, "come git aboard. We're a-haulin' back to Dep'ford in a hurry!"

Dan ran back and picked up the musket, then clambered to the box. Deftly manipulating his reins, the fat driver pulled the leaders around and succeeded in turning the sled in the narrow compass of the road. When they were headed east once more, he snapped the long lash savagely over the horses' backs and sent them down the hill at a headlong gallop.

SIXTEEN

NATE GILMAN was too busy, during most of that wild ride, to pay much attention to the miserable lad beside him. And Dan, sunk in dejection, had no inclination to break the silence between them. After a few miles of strenuous driving, however, the coachman's disgruntled mood wore off.

"Don't ye go blamin' yerself, boy," he said, not unkindly. " 'Twas more my fault than yours, fer I should ha' stayed awake. An' goodness knows a gun don't always go off when ye want it to."

"Frost got in the primin', I guess," the unhappy Dan replied. "But if I'd looked at it oftener, an' told you when I heard that hoss snort—"

"Well, what's done is done," said the driver. "Can't be helped now, an' it ain't as bad as it might be. There was a mail-sack half full o' paper money that they missed. Wuth twice as much as the silver in the box. Wisht I knowed who them ruffians was, though."

Dan leaned forward eagerly. "I b'lieve I know one of

'em, anyway," he said. "You remember that night at the tavern—the man in the bell-crowned hat that tried to rob the till an' got away on the big black hoss?"

"Sure!" exclaimed Gilman. "Dog my cats if he ain't the same one! The feller that kep' the pistol on us. I oughta knowed that handsome black nag o' his the minute I laid eyes on him!"

"It's Cap'n Hairtrigger, all right," Dan said. "But there's another of 'em I've got a feelin' I've seen somewhere. That big rough one that yanked me off the seat. He had a hoarse sort of voice an' I'd swear I've heard it before. Can't think where it could ha' been, though."

They were galloping into the village now. Dan told the coachman about the vigilance committee. "If you stop at Ben Tucker's," he said, "he'll send 'round an' git men an' hosses together."

Accordingly Gilman pulled his panting team to a halt before the blacksmith shop and blew a tremendous blast on the cow-horn.

In an upper window of the house beside the forge, Ben Tucker's head and burly shoulders appeared. "What's the trouble?" he bellowed.

"It's the stage," the fat driver answered. "Three men held us up on the road an' robbed the mails. Got off with a box o' money. One of 'em looked like this Cap'n Hairtrigger!"

"Ye don't say!" cried the blacksmith. "Where'bouts was it?"

"Not more'n five mile up the road. They was mounted, an' I reckon they took to the woods."

"I'll git the boys out right away," called Tucker, preparing to shut the window. "Who's that on the seat with ye?"

"It's me—Dan Drew," the boy replied.

"Good! Dan, you git a hoss from Skilly an' go up to Newt Nixon's, quick as ye kin make it. Tell him what's happened an' send him down here with what men he kin pick up along the road. We'll be makin' a start 'fore daylight!"

With that he ducked back inside and they could see the flicker of a lighted candle through the window as the horses plunged forward again.

The tavern looked dark and silent from the road, but when they came to a jingling stop in the yard, the kitchen door was thrown open. Maria Bassett had not gone back to bed after the stage's departure. She was up and getting a good start on her baking.

"My land o' Goshen!" cried the good woman, throwing her hands aloft. "What's happened?"

They told her as quickly as they could, while the shivering passengers left the stage to crowd around the kitchen fire.

"An' Ben Tucker wants me to go fer Newt Nixon," Dan put in. "Do you s'pose there's a hoss I kin take?"

"I swan, I don't know!" the flustered landlady replied. "With the mare stole, an' the sorrel gone lame yestiddy, there ain't a thing left in the barn. Skilly's still asleep but I'll call him if ye want."

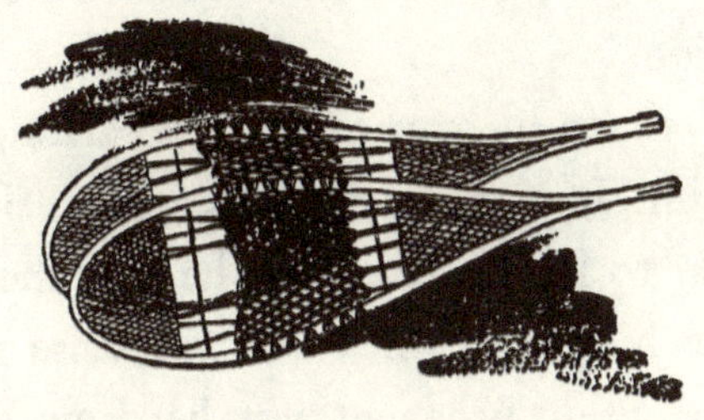

"Well, maybe he ought to know 'bout the robbery," Dan answered. "But I'll start anyhow. I can make just as good time if I go 'cross country on my snowshoes."

The gray half-light of the false dawn was stealing through the woods as he began his journey. The way to the clearing was fairly familiar to him now and he jogged on steadily with no pause to take his bearings. Far off in the valley the roosters were beginning to crow. He would have to hurry if he wanted to bring Nixon word of the hold-up in time to join the posse.

When he had been traveling fast for twenty minutes or more it came to him that he had never followed this exact route before. His general direction was right, he knew, but he had passed no recognizable landmarks. Had he strayed too far eastward or westward to come out on the clearing? There was no way to tell but to keep moving ahead, and before he had gone many more yards his question was answered. Faintly, through the woods, he heard a ferocious barking of dogs. The sound came at an angle from the left and he bent his steps in that direction.

At intervals, as he hurried on, the barking continued to guide him. It was much nearer now. Just as daybreak began to lighten the east, he saw the trees thinning before him, and knew he was close to the edge of the open field. When at last he drew clear of the woods the buildings had a strange look. From where he stood he could not see the house—only the roofs of a barn and a shed, rising beyond a great heap of brush. Then he realized that changing his course had brought him into the clearing from the back. He would have to go around the buildings.

Dan moved cautiously now, for he had no wish to be set upon by the dogs till he was in sight of the house door. He was just skirting the edge of the brush-pile when he heard a voice shouting. A queer, deep, husky voice—like a man's but somehow different. Big Liz—or was it? An appalling flash of understanding stopped the boy in his tracks. The robber who had knocked him down, two hours ago, was the giant wife of Newt Nixon! There was no mistaking that voice, now that he heard it again!

For several seconds Dan stood there, his brain in a whirl. The shock of his discovery had left him powerless to move. But in another moment he knew he had to act, and act quickly. The woman was coming nearer, cursing at every step and calling for Newt. She must be almost past the corner of the barn now.

Slipping off his snowshoes, Dan dove into the edge of the brush-heap like a scared rabbit. He pulled the shoes in after him, hiding them under the mass of twigs, then crept farther toward the middle of the pile. The snow was soft and deep, and he burrowed along in silence, trying desperately not to crackle the branches over his head.

He heard Big Liz shout once more—this time only a few yards away. What if she should find his snowshoe tracks! He held his breath through seconds that seemed like years. And at last the huge woman went muttering away again. Dan listened till he was sure she had returned to the house, then grinned a shaky grin to himself. His body was drenched with sweat and he was trembling like a leaf.

He wiped his forehead with his mitten. Now he knew what he had to do and there wasn't a minute to be lost.

If he could get back to Ben Tucker's before the troop
set out, he could tell them just where to find their highwaymen. Crawling out the way he had come, he found
himself sinking deeper into the snow. Suddenly there
was a soft, rushing sound beneath him and his feet shot
downward. Before he could stretch out his arms he was
falling through smothering darkness.

The boy landed with jarring force on a hard surface
ten feet below. The wind was knocked out of him, but
as soon as he had his breath again he moved his arms and
legs and found himself uninjured. Gradually his eyes became accustomed to the dim light that came from the
hole above him. The floor on which he sat seemed to be
of trampled earth. Overhead was a roof of poles and
brush. One of the poles had broken under his weight
and he had fallen through the narrow opening.

It was warm in this underground cavern, he found.
Around him, unseen in the dark, he could hear soft
rustlings and munchings, and there was a pungent smell
of horses in the close air. He got to his feet and took
a step or two, groping his way with outstretched hands.
On one side of him was a pile of hay or straw, and beyond it several covered chests of grain. A row of stalls
occupied the other side of the subterranean stable. There
were four or five horses standing there, but he could
tell little about their size or color.

In one end of the place—the end nearest the barn, he thought—there was a broad plank door. He tried it and found it fastened from the other side. If he meant to get out at all, it would have to be through the roof, the way he had come in.

The aperture between the poles was a good five feet above his head. He looked in the grain-bins and found one which was only partly filled. It was still heavy, but by straining and tugging he was able to move it a few inches at a time. Finally it was in position under the hole and he mounted hurriedly to the broad lid. Reaching upward he discovered that his fingers still missed the poles by a foot. But perhaps if he jumped he could get a hand-hold. Crouching and balancing himself he started an upward spring. *Crash!* The flimsy top of the grain-box gave way beneath him and he fell sprawling. The startled horses snorted and kicked in their stalls, making a deafening racket. And just as their noise was subsiding, his ears caught another sound. Someone was removing the bar that secured the door of his dungeon!

Dan lay still behind his grain chest, hardly daring to breathe. He heard the door creak open. A heavy tread came slowly across the earthen floor and the rays of a lantern lit up the row of stalls. Frightened as he was, the boy's eyes missed no detail of the scene around him. The first stall was empty, he saw. But in the next one the

lantern-light glinted on a sleek bay rump that he would
have recognized anywhere. It was Skilly Bassett's little
mare, Lady!

For a moment, the footsteps seemed to move away.
Then he heard a muttered exclamation of surprise.
"What the devil! How'd them oats git over there?"

The lantern flickered quickly nearer and flashed down
directly in his face. Half-blinded he stared up at the
red whiskers and cold, pale eyes of Newt Nixon. For a
moment neither of them spoke. There was surprise in
the backwoodsman's hard face, and a trace of something
like fear. He looked upward quickly at the broken roof-

pole, then back at the boy again. "We-ell," he drawled, a vindictive grin twisting the corners of his mouth. "The young snooper's been at it again, huh? Thought ye'd stick yer nose in other folks' business, an' fell plumb through the roof! Ha-ha!"

The laugh had no mirth in it. Stooping quickly, Nixon seized Dan's wrist and jerked him to his feet.

"What brung ye here?" he asked, with an ugly edge to his voice.

The boy swallowed, trying to speak calmly. "They sent me from the village," he said, "to fetch you quick as you can come. There's been a robbery, an' the committee's gettin' ready to ride."

"Oh, that was the way of it, huh?" sneered the bearded man. "An' ye thought the short cut to the house was through the brush-pile?" He paused to give Dan's wrist a vicious twist. "Well, I got a way to fix the likes o' you, young feller! Come along now an' let's see if we can't find a snugger place fer ye!"

At once he started dragging Dan toward the entrance of the underground stable. They passed through, Nixon kicking the door shut behind him, and made their way between barrels and boxes that nearly filled a second chamber, dug out of the earth like the first. The goods stored there looked like the cargoes of freight-wagons and pod-auger sleds—stolen plunder, if Dan guessed correctly. But he had little time to examine the place.

In one corner an inclined ramp of heavy planks sloped upward to what appeared to be a huge trap-door. Nixon pulled him past this, and along a narrow tunnel that extended several yards to the left. At the end of the passage a rude ladder was fastened, and above it was another trap-door, small and square. Mounting to the first rung of the ladder, the man pounded with his fist on the underside of the trap.

"Who's there?" came a guarded voice from above.

"It's me—Newt. I got a surprise fer ye, Liz! Open up, can't ye?"

The floor creaked under heavy feet and the trap-door was lifted. Pale daylight came through the opening. Nixon shoved Dan ahead of him up the ladder. "Git on up there with ye, an' let the old lady have a look at what I found!" he chuckled grimly. And white-faced and stumbling, the boy crawled out of the hole to find himself standing in the kitchen of the farm-house.

Opposite him, a couple of paces away, the terrifying figure of Big Liz loomed huge and shadowy in the gray light of early morning. She still had on the homespun breeches and boots she had worn during the raid on the mail-stage. The mass of her sandy hair was pulled into a knot at the back of her head, and with her slouched hat off there was no mistaking her sex. Dan saw the coarse lips curl back from her long yellow teeth in a snarl that was more animal than human.

She pointed her finger at him. "How'd he git here?" she asked her husband hoarsely. Nixon pulled himself up from the opening and slammed down the trap.

"Spyin' again, I reckon," he scowled. "Must ha' been crawlin' 'round in that brush-heap back o' the barn an' fell into the cellar. One thing sure—we can't be bothered with him now. Too much goin' on. What d'ye say? Knock him in the head?"

Dan flinched in spite of himself at those words. Big Liz, watching him as a cat would a mouse, saw the involuntary quiver of his body and a cruel smile spread over her features.

"Naw," she chuckled. "Let him wait fer it a spell. We kin tie him up good an' stick him up in the loft where he won't be in the way. When this blows over it'll be time enough to settle his hash. Git that spare bed-cord that's in the shed."

The red-bearded man went out obediently and the giantess stood eying her prisoner. "So I didn't wallop ye hard enough back there on the road?" she growled softly. "By 'mighty, the nex' time I'll break yer neck!"

Dan stiffened his jaw and faced her stoutly. His fear was giving way before a rising temper. He half wished she would swing that heavy fist again, for he knew he was quicker than she. However, before any violence could happen, Newt Nixon returned from his errand. He stepped up back of the boy and pinioned his arms from behind. Quickly and effectively, he whipped a dozen strands of quarter-inch hemp around Dan's wrists and elbows.

"Lie down!" he ordered, and when the boy hesitated, he was tripped heavily, falling on his side. In another moment his ankles also were securely bound. Then a ball of dirty cloth was forced between his jaws and tied firmly in place for a gag. Helpless, he lay there and stared stoically up at his captors.

"Take his legs," said Big Liz, at the same time gripping him by the shoulders. "Now—up with him!"

Dan was carried through some sort of dark hallway and hoisted up a slanting ladder. At the top there was another trap-door with a stout hasp to fasten it. Chilly air struck his face as he entered the darkness of the attic. They dumped him down on the boards and left him there. He could hear Big Liz's hoarse laugh as they closed and fastened the trap.

"Reckon he'll keep safe enough," she said. "Leave him lay till we kin 'tend to him right."

SEVENTEEN

DAN'S first action, after the Nixons left him alone in the cold and dark of the attic, was a vigorous attempt to free his arms and legs. For nearly half an hour he struggled, tugging with all his strength at the stout new rope. But it appeared that the red-bearded robber knew his business. He had tied those bonds with an expert hand. There was no way in which the boy could get his fingers on the knots, and pulling in any direction merely caused the rope to bite deeper into his wrists. When finally he gave up trying, the skin was so cruelly chafed that it was hard for him to keep from crying out with pain.

Lying on his side, exhausted with effort, he tried to think out some logical plan of escape. If he remained where he was he had no doubt about his fate. He knew too much to be allowed to live. Newt Nixon might hesitate to put him out of the way, but he felt that Big Liz would be utterly ruthless.

Meanwhile, even if he should succeed in getting his

hands free, there was no way he could see to break out of the garret. His only hope, then, lay in being released by his friends in Deptford. He tried to figure what was happening in the village. The posse must already have ridden off from the blacksmith shop, galloping out the west road, hunting for the bandits' trail. If they found it he had no confidence that it could be followed long. There were too many by-ways, packed hard by horses' hooves, where the track might be lost.

It would be many hours, he thought, before anyone remembered his errand and began wondering what had become of him. At the tavern they would suppose he had joined the troop and was out scouring the country-side for the highwaymen. Ben Tucker would take it for granted he was back at the inn. All in all, his situation was far from hopeful.

Dan was too tired now to care. He had been up since half-past three and his brain was numb with fatigue. Gradually he relaxed, his head resting on the floor, and drowsed off into a troubled sleep.

Several hours must have passed before he woke again. At first he could not remember where he was, but the harsh jerk of the ropes reminded him as soon as he tried to move. It was still day-time outside. He could see faint lines of light coming through chinks between the timbers. Downstairs there were voices and a rattle of dishes. A meal must be in progress. Hitching himself along the boards, a little at a time, he found a narrow crack in the flooring that permitted him to see part of the kitchen below.

One end of a deal table was in sight and on it plates of steaming food. The smell of hot roast beef came faintly up through the crack and made the hungry lad's mouth water. He wondered if his jailers would give him anything to eat. Occasionally he could see a hand and part of a sleeve move above the food, plying a steel knife and fork. There was little conversation. What few remarks were made seemed to be commonplaces concerning the weather and the chances of a person called "Mike" getting to some place or other before the roads were blocked. As nearly as Dan could determine there were only two people in the room below—Newt Nixon and his huge wife. They spoke to each other in surly monosyllables. There were a few curses but no humor and no kindliness in their talk.

Finally a chair scraped back and heavy feet tramped across the kitchen. "Goin' to tend the stock," the red-beard mumbled, and Dan heard him belching comfortably as he started for the barn. Now, perhaps, Big Liz would remember her prisoner and feed him. But no—she was carrying the plates to the wash-pan, on a bench by the fire. He heard water poured into the pan from the kettle, followed by the slosh and rattle that attended dish-washing. Then a chunk of wood was thrown into the flames and the giantess moved off to another room, humming to herself monotonously under her breath.

Dan was no longer sleepy, much as he wished he could sleep. There was nothing to do but lie still and try to forget his misery while the endless afternoon wore away. For a long time the house was quiet. Distant sounds came from the outbuildings, where Newt Nixon was apparently still at work, but Dan thought Big Liz must be asleep. After her night's marauding he could understand why. Perhaps they were going out after plunder again tonight!

It had occurred to him as strange that he had seen nothing of the black horse's rider. Certainly he had been the third member of the band that morning. Dan had a vivid memory of the trio as they rode off over the hill. The man with the pistol had been leading the pack-horse, he remembered. Had the gang split up after they were out of sight? Had his old acquaintance, Captain Hairtrigger, taken the stolen money to some other hiding-place, farther away? And this "Mike" the Nixons had mentioned—could that be still another of the captain's many names?

Puzzling over these things made Dan's head throb painfully. He was dizzy—a little feverish, he thought.

And now thirst had been added to his other tortures. His throat was so dry that he could scarcely swallow.

Lying there in a half-doze, he was roused suddenly by the neighing of a horse, outside in the clearing. Soon there was a thud of hooves close to the house. With a

struggle the boy raised himself to a sitting position, listening hopefully. Three slow knocks sounded on the door. He heard Big Liz shuffle across the kitchen and throw back the bolt. With her first words the lad's heart sank again.

"Oh, it's you, Lafe," she said. "Well, git that hoss out o' sight. Newt's out to the barn. He'll open up fer ye."

Ten minutes later the two men came in by way of the trap in the kitchen floor. The one called Lafe was talking. His voice was unfamiliar to Dan and the brief glimpse the boy caught of him through the floor-crack showed him a small, shabby man with unkempt gray whiskers—a man he couldn't recall seeing around the village.

"Whew!" the fellow was saying. "Shore was ticklish business gittin' 'round on the roads today! Riders thicker'n huckleberries as fur up as Half Moon. . . . Yeah —he got through. Not much to spare, though. One bunch missed him by half a minute when he jumped the wall. Never noticed his tracks an' rode right by. . . . No, I don't reckon he'll move from there 'fore dark tomorrer—wants to let things settle down a mite."

"Well," came Big Liz's rumbling answer, "all that sounds good enough. Soon as I give ye somethin' to eat, Lafe, ye'd better lay low in the dug-out. No tellin'. We might have visitors tonight."

Dusk had fallen, and soon a tallow candle was lighted in the kitchen. Dan could hear preparations for supper going on. Once more the smell of cooking food reached his nostrils. He groaned behind the filthy rag that filled his dry mouth, and rolled over so that he could no longer be tantalized.

After a while his ears told him the three people in the room below had finished their meal. Lafe said goodnight and the trap-door slammed after him.

There was an interval while Dan must have drowsed

again, for he did not hear the barking of the dogs or the horses trotting into the yard. His first knowledge of a new arrival was when a loud hammering at the door brought him up, wide awake.

"Who's there?" called Newt Nixon, and the boy heard the constable's high, squeaky voice answer, outside.

"It's me—Asa Pease—an' some o' the committee."

"Well, I'll be durned!" cried the red-whiskered man heartily, as he opened the door. "What's up? You fellers jest ridin' fer the fun of it? Come in, won't ye?"

"Reckon we can't," returned the fat officer of the law. "Late fer supper at home now. We was wonderin' why you didn't show up this mornin'. Mail was robbed an' we been scourin' round on the trail o' the rascals since sun-up. Didn't that boy let ye know 'bout it?"

"Me? Why, no!" exclaimed Nixon in loud surprise. "We ain't seen no boy round here, have we, Ma? First I'd heard about the robbery. Did ye git 'em?"

"Naw," was the disgusted reply from half a dozen of the men outside. "Rode till we was saddle-sore. . . . Struck their trail an' then lost it. . . . You had it easy, Newt, settin' home all day!"

Nixon's roar of laughter was full of good humor. "By golly," he said, "if I'd knowed ye was bein' called out, I shore wouldn't ha' missed it fer money! Are ye figgerin' on goin' again tomorrer?"

"Don't see what good it'd do," Pease returned sourly. "We've searched about everywheres. An' these boys have their work to do, besides. Reckon we'll have to give up."

Dan thought he detected a note of relief in the big backwoodsman's voice when he answered. "Well," he called out, "let me know if I'm needed, an' I'll be right on deck. Good-night, all!"

They were leaving! Mustering all his strength, the boy tried to shout for help. But all it amounted to was a faint, gargling bleat, strangled by the gag. He knew, bitterly, that it would never reach the ears of the posse, already turning their horses to ride away.

He had not realized till that moment how high his hopes had risen. Now that they were shattered once more he could hardly hold back the tears of disappointment. In all his life he had never felt so helpless or so lonely.

The evening wore along and the kitchen below was dark and silent. As the fire died, the meager warmth that had come up through the attic floor-boards gave place to biting cold. Dan hitched his way across the narrow garret to lie with his back to the big chimney. The rough stones still held a little heat.

In spite of the thirst and hunger that tormented him,

he felt a drowsiness coming over his senses. Soon he fell into a restless dreaming, on the borderland of sleep. Queer shapes and scenes that had a frightening reality spun fantastically through his fevered brain. In one of them Dr. Barlow, with a wicked-looking surgical knife in his hand, and a cruel leer on his thin lips, was standing over him. The lips moved as if the man were uttering horrible threats, yet there was no sound of a voice. Dan's muscles jerked in a frantic effort to escape, and the movement woke him.

The doctor! It was strange that until that moment the boy had not thought about the sinister Barlow in connection with his present predicament. Yet he had seen the little bay mare that morning in the underground stable! Desperately he tried to fit together the pieces of his puzzle. What did the doctor have to do with the Nixons—with Hairtrigger—and the rest of the robber band? Had he been held up? Murdered, perhaps, and the horse stolen? But if that were so, what had become of the poor little orphan, Dolores?

Such questions were more than his weary mind could cope with. He gave up after a time and lay relaxed, drifting into dreams again.

. . . .

There was a glimmer of daylight through the chinks when Dan woke. He felt queer and light-headed, and his arms and legs, cramped from lying all night in one position, no longer seemed to belong to him. When he moved, however, he soon discovered his limbs were still there. As the numbness left them, it was replaced by sheer agony.

The attic was bitterly cold. He could hear the crackle of a new fire on the hearth but it had not yet warmed through the chimney stones. The chill seemed to have penetrated deep into his body. Again and again he shivered till his teeth rattled. For one moment of utter despair he wished his captors would come up and finish him—get it over with.

Just then, from below, came a new sound that startled him. Temporarily he forgot his troubles and crouched, listening with rapt attention. The sound was indistinct at first, hardly louder than the mewing of a kitten. Then the door to another room must have been opened, for he heard it more plainly. Sobs! The pitiful voice of a child, crying as if in desolation.

Newt Nixon spoke gruffly from the kitchen. "Shut her up, can't ye?" And in the next breath Dan heard Big Liz's growl. She seemed to be in a different part of the house but her words, low and fierce, were audible enough.

"Hush yer mouth!" she said. "Stop that bawlin' or I'll

mash ye flat. . . . No, he ain't. Yer paw won't be back till night!"

With that, a door slammed noisily. The sobbing had ceased and the house was quiet once more.

EIGHTEEN

IN Dan's half-conscious state, the happenings of that morning made a blurred, strange pattern that he could never recall with any clearness. He could remember dimly hearing a pounding somewhere below, and the lifting of the trap-door to admit the man they called Lafe. While breakfast was being eaten, a long conversation went on below. Only a few of the words he heard made any impression on the boy's numb brain. But once an arresting phrase or two caught his attention.

Lafe had been rambling on and on between mouthfuls of food. Suddenly he struck his fist on the table and made a remark that Dan could take in. "Way I look at it," he said, "we got to find a new way to git the stuff to Canada. Mebbe over through Vermont—I dunno. But anyhow them roads north o' here ain't safe, night or day, no more."

Newt Nixon's reply was unintelligible, but the boy had heard enough. The word "Canada" touched off the spark. He knew now, as plainly as if he had been told,

that he had fallen into the hands of the "Stingers"—
that dreaded band of thieves who operated all the way
from the middle states to the northern border!

Another memory he had was of Lafe's departure,
hours later.

"Take the back trail," Newt Nixon was telling him.
"Ye won't see a soul till ye hit the Half Moon road.
Tell him the coast's clear now. If he don't start till dusk
he'll git here without a speck o' trouble."

That, Dan thought hazily, must be the man they
called "Mike." Captain Hairtrigger, perhaps. Or perhaps the father of the child he had heard crying at daybreak. Hadn't Big Liz said something like "yer paw
won't be back till night"? Funny, he thought, that he
should have jumped at the idea the baby might be
Dolores! It couldn't be, of course, if it had a father.
And yet when he first heard those sobs he had been
almost certain . . .

A heavy sleep engulfed him and he lay like a log until
past noon. When he woke at last he was weak and faint
but his head was surprisingly clear. He moved his legs
a little, to bring back the circulation, but otherwise he
remained quiet, conserving his strength. As nearly as he
could figure, he had been in the garret now for more
than thirty hours. Once, in Portsmouth, a sailor had
told him about being adrift in a small boat without food

or water for nine days. Perhaps, Dan thought, he could live that long, but he doubted it. The ropes, and the gag in his mouth, would make it harder. On the other hand, he reflected, it didn't seem likely that he would be left in his prison indefinitely. Perhaps the evil pair downstairs were only waiting for their partner to return—tonight.

There was only one chance for him if he wanted to live. Somehow he must get his hands free. His eyes had become used to the dim light of the attic now, and with cool deliberation he looked about for something that would help him. At last his glance fell on the chimney, built into the end of the house. At one corner of the masonry he saw a stone with a rough edge!

It took the boy several minutes to hoist himself into a position where he could feel the jutting rock with his hands. His wrists were cut so deeply by the rope, and his fingers were so puffed and swollen, that every movement brought him intense pain. But in spite of it he began to rub the strands of hemp up and down against the sharp granite.

A little of this was all that he could stand at a time. In less than a minute he was forced to slump on the floor, gasping and exhausted. He rested there, gathering his strength, and tried again. This time he felt something give a trifle. One ply of the rope must have frayed through. He was bracing himself for a third attempt when the dogs set up a sudden frenzied barking outside.

Between their yelps he could hear Big Liz and her husband talking in low, excited voices.

"Who is it—kin ye see?" the woman asked.

"Yeah—seems to be Ben Tucker an' three or four others. I don't like the look o' this, Liz! He's carryin' a gun!"

"Gun, eh? Gimme that cordwood stick an' I'll bat his brains in—the sneakin' louse—"

"Hold on, woman—are ye daft?" Nixon muttered. "There's too many of 'em fer that. Thing fer us to do is leave the door barred an' git under ground quick! They'll leave if they think we ain't here."

Dan heard the trap lifted stealthily, and just at that moment a loud banging began on the door. "Open up, there, Newt Nixon," roared the blacksmith. "We're a-comin' in, an' we don't aim to fool around."

The silence that followed lasted a dozen heartbeats. Then Tucker's determined bass rumbled again. "All right," he said, "we're breakin' down the door!"

Almost at once there was a thunderous crash that made the whole house tremble. When it came again, Dan heard a rending of splintered wood. Once more, and the bar broke, letting the door fly inward.

Then heavy feet tramped the floor below. "Don't

seem to be home, do they?" said the smith. "Might be hidin' in one o' these rooms, though. Go careful, but don't miss a closet or a corner."

Dan knew he could never make his voice heard above the noise of their search. He rolled over on his back and lifted his bound feet, bringing them down on the boards as hard as he could.

"Hold on!" called Tucker. "Thought I heard a noise—sort of a thumpin'."

Again the boy struck his boot-heels on the floor.

"There!" he heard the blacksmith exclaim. "By hokus, I b'lieve it come from up-attic! Hey—Dan! Dan Drew!"

For a moment there was silence. They were waiting—expecting him to answer. Dan filled his lungs and did his best to shout. The sound of his half-smothered voice must have reached Ben Tucker's ears, for he called back at once. "All right, Danny—we'll find ye!"

New energy seemed to flow through the boy's weakened frame at those encouraging words. He rolled and wriggled along the boards till he reached the trap-door and pounded on it with his heels. Somebody was in the passage below. Then climbing the ladder! The iron hasp was flung back and the trap began to open, letting a gust of warm air into the attic. And no sight had ever been more welcome to the imprisoned lad than the bearded face and mighty shoulders of Ben Tucker, as he thrust himself up through the opening.

The blacksmith blinked for a moment, unaccustomed to the darkness. Then he saw Dan move and quickly hoisted himself up to sit on the edge of the flooring. As he became aware of the boy's condition, a growl of anger and pity rumbled in his throat. He whipped out a clasp-knife. "Steady, lad," he said. "I'll have ye free in a second."

The gag dropped away from Dan's mouth and he gulped gratefully at a mouthful of clean air. Then his numbed and swollen hands were free. It was all he could do to move his arms forward into a natural position, so long had they been cramped behind him.

"Ben!" he croaked through parched lips. "Did they git away?"

"Who—Newt an' Big Liz? Not yet, they didn't! I reckon we got 'em pretty well bottled up. Here—don't try to talk now. Lemme git a comfortable holt an' I'll have ye downstairs in a jiffy."

Dan swayed dizzily when he tried to stand up, in the kitchen. Ben set him in a chair and brought a dipper of water from the bucket that stood by the window-ledge. The boy drank, a little at a time, his dry mouth reveling in the moisture and coolness. As he put the dipper down, Tucker grinned at him.

"Feel better, don't ye?" he asked. "Now, then, soon as ye kin talk, tell me—any idee where that pair o' hulkin' rats might ha' hid out?"

Before Dan could answer, there was a sound of running feet. Through the door from the next room burst Ethan Hayes, his freckled face shining with excitement. "Hey—guess who we found, Ben!" he panted. Then he caught sight of his chum and let out a whoop of joy.

"Are ye all right, Dan?" he asked, seizing him by the shoulders. "Gosh! I was scairt to death somethin' had happened to ye!"

"Hold on," the blacksmith interrupted. "What was it ye said ye found?"

"Why, that little young 'un the doctor stole— Dolores! She was hid in a crib in the bedroom—with a curtain in front of it to make it look like a closet—"

At that moment Amos Crandall appeared, carrying the child in his arms. His kindly face had a grim look. "Thank the Lord," he said soberly, "she's still alive. She's been mistreated, though. Poor little soul—look how she's tremblin' now!"

Dan stared at the child. It *had* been Dolores he had heard crying that morning! She was so thin and pale he would scarcely have known her. And though she was looking at him now, there was no recognition in her drawn, frightened little face.

"That child's in need of some real care," said Ben Tucker, gently. "We've got enough men here, Amos. You git her in the sleigh an' put out fer home, fast as ye kin!"

Through the window, Dan watched Crandall carry his light burden out to a waiting cutter. Near it, he saw, were half a dozen saddle-horses, tethered to the barn-yard fence. Two young troopers from the village stood guard with guns in their hands. One of them he recognized as Ethan's brother, Elijah. The other was a lad named Joe Blake.

"Now," growled the blacksmith, "let's git on with this. Where are they, Dan?"

The boy pointed across the kitchen to the trap-door in the floor. "There's a dug-out cave back there under the barn," he said. "I fell into it. That's how they caught me."

Tucker nodded. "We guessed it. Ol' Gunticus follered yer tracks through the woods an' told us where they ended up. I've got three good men posted 'round that brush-pile. Think there's any other way they could git out?"

"Yes," said Dan. "There's a runway fer hosses leadin' up to a big trap-door that must open in the barn."

"Hm," the smith frowned. "So there's three places to watch, instead o' two. I'd better tell the boys outside to keep an eye on the barn door."

He had his hand on the latch when a yell broke from one of the guards outside. "Look!" cried Ethan. "The barn door's openin' now!"

Dan reached the window in time to see the big door swing wide. Out of the gaping darkness leaped a horse, with a bulky shape crouched low on its back. A second mounted figure followed on the heels of the first.

"Shoot!" yelled Ben Tucker. But before the troopers

in the yard could level their guns, Newt Nixon blazed away with a pistol and young Blake dropped wounded in the snow. Elijah Hayes kept his presence of mind. Even as the red-bearded outlaw galloped past him he fired his musket at point-blank range. Nixon swayed and fell to the ground.

Big Liz by now was nearly a hundred yards off, across the clearing. Dan saw Ethan standing in the doorway, resting his rifle against the jamb. He sighted coolly, and the sharp crack of the shot echoed deafeningly in the kitchen. The horse ridden by the woman seemed to stumble, then regain its stride. But the gallop had changed to a limping trot.

"You hit the hoss!" shouted Tucker. "Stay here with Dan—I'm goin' after her!"

He swung into the saddle and spurred his mount in whirlwind pursuit. The guard who had been hit yelled something to Elijah, who ran toward the wounded robber. Dan saw him stoop down to feel Nixon's breast. Suddenly the still form on the ground moved. A big arm shot out and caught the trooper by the neck. Ethan flung aside his empty rifle and dashed to the aid of his brother. The outlaw could not have been seriously hurt, for he was fighting with bearlike ferocity. And though his young assailants hung on like a couple of terriers, Dan could see that the battle was going against them.

Frantic, he looked around for Ethan's powder-flask and bullets. They were nowhere in sight. In a flash of desperation, the boy staggered to the door and picked up the rifle.

How he got across the yard he never knew, for his head was reeling and his knees buckled under him. But somehow he made it. The big red-beard was on his feet

now, holding Ethan by the throat and struggling to shake off the grip of the other lad from his arm.

Dan braced his legs and lifted the empty gun. "Let go, Nixon!" he cried. "Put up yer hands, 'fore I blow yer head off!"

The bluff worked. Newt Nixon's vindictive eyes stared at the unwavering muzzle of the rifle—then at the white, set face of the boy who aimed it. His strangle-hold on Ethan's throat relaxed. Slowly he raised his hands above his head.

"Take off yer belt, Ethan," Dan said, never shifting his gaze from the ruffian in front of him. "Tie his hands good an' solid. 'Lije—there's a rope in the kitchen—the one he used on me. That'll hold him, I reckon."

It was all he could do to get the last words out. The rifle was growing unbearably heavy in his hands and he felt himself swaying like a cornstalk in the wind. "That's the way—tie him up—good!" he panted through clenched teeth. And in another moment he crumpled slowly earthward. A black void of unconsciousness engulfed him.

' ' ' '

When Dan came to, a few minutes later, he was looking up into Ethan's anxious face. The boy saw his eyes open and grinned with relief. "Gosh, Dan!" he said. "You scairt the gizzard out o' me—goin' off like that. I been rubbin' ye with snow fer I dunno how long!"

"He didn't—get away, did he?" whispered Dan.

"Shucks, no! He's trussed up like a pig in a sack! 'Lije's bullet got him in the muscle o' the neck. Jest a flesh-wound but he's bleedin' a good bit. Joe Blake ain't hurt bad, either. Collar-bone busted, I reckon. The other fellers come from back o' the barn an' carried 'em both inside."

"Who else is here?" Dan asked.

"Why, Tim Garrity an' Gunticus an' another feller from Ben's troop. They was watchin' around that brush-heap. Tim's gone to help Tucker. Say—here they come now! An' holy smokes! They've got Big Liz!"

Turning his head, Dan could see two horses approaching at a walk, and one of them carried a double burden. Big Liz Nixon hung like a huge meal-sack across Ben Tucker's saddle-bow.

Tim kicked his horse and trotted ahead as they drew nearer. "How's Danny comin' on?" he called. And then, "Begob, it's awake he is!"

The hostler swung down from the saddle and bent over Dan, grinning a wide Irish grin. "Ye look like a ghost, boy!" he said. "How long is it since ye had a bite o' food?"

"I dunno," Dan answered. "Must be two days, I guess."

"Jeepers!" growled Garrity. "The swine niver fed ye? Here, Ethan, skip in the house an' rustle some grub fer the lad. I'll carry him meself."

Within ten minutes, Dan was sipping a cup of hot milk in the kitchen. Around him the men from the village stood or sprawled, discussing the results of their raid. Tim Garrity was regaling them with an account of Big Liz's capture.

"Ah," he said, " 'twas as foine a sight as ye'd wish to see! A scrap betwixt a pair of elephints wouldn't be one—two—three wid it! They're both off their horses whin I come up, an' both rushin' at each other like wild bulls. The woman swings a haymaker at Ben's head fit

to knock down a house, but Ben ducks just in time.
Then he grabs her an' down they go wid a crash like a
tree fallin'. Liz is on top, gougin' at his eyes wid both
thumbs. A pity, thinks I—'tis the last poor Ben'll iver
see o' the light o' day! But, bedad, he squirms from
under an' they're both up again, fast as cats! Ochone, I
sez to meself, if he on'y had his blacksmith's sledge in
his fist, now! Old Ben'd niver strike a lady, o' course,
but that gougin' must ha' taught him this was no lady.
Annyway, he let fly, an' I knew he didn't need no
sledge. The crack he give her on the jaw would ha' flat-
tened an iron bar. I helped him pick her up, an' I'll
swear to it she weighs not an ounce under three hundred
pound!"

Tucker looked red-faced and sheepish. " 'Twan't
quite as desp'rit as all that," he mumbled. "But if I
hadn't happened to git mad, I swan I dunno how it
might ha' finished up."

He turned to Dan. "How d'ye feel by now, lad?" he
asked. "Ready fer some real grub?"

The boy shook his head. "Guess I'd better stick to
milk," he smiled. "I'm feelin' a lot stronger, though.
Where's Gunticus? I'd like to thank him for bringin'
you here."

"That's right—where is the old Injun?" Ethan asked.
"He was right here a minute ago."

"Look in the front room," suggested Ben Tucker. "Thought I saw him headin' in there."

A moment later they heard the farmer boy let out a whoop of merriment. Then there was a shuffling of moccasined feet and Ethan pushed the old Indian before him into the kitchen. Gunticus was carrying a small stone jug in one hand. In the other he held a black surgical case. And perched owlishly on his copper-colored nose was a pair of dark spectacles.

While the others roared with laughter, Dan leaned forward, gasping in surprise. Those spectacles—that black case! They were Dr. Barlow's!

"Ben!" he cried, remembering. "Did you go through that underground barn o' theirs? Skilly Bassett's mare is in there—the one the doctor took! An' here's his bag an' glasses. That's why you found Dolores here. Don't you see? He's mixed up in this somehow!"

"Ye don't say!" the blacksmith replied, sobering. "Skilly's Lady mare? Boys, we better git down in there an' see what else they stole. It's gittin' on towards night an' we'll want to be leavin' soon."

"Wait!" Dan exclaimed. "There's somethin' I forgot to tell you. This mornin' I heard 'em talk about another one o' their gang. I think his name's Mike. Anyway he's supposed to be comin' down here from Half Moon as soon as it's dark!"

Ben Tucker thought a moment and slapped his thigh. "Good!" he ejaculated. "Couldn't be better! We'll put the hosses out o' sight an' wait fer him right here! Might as well round up the whole kaboodle of 'em at one crack."

NINETEEN

GATHERING dusk crept slowly into the quiet kitchen. The embers crackled with a soft, pleasant sound on the hearth. While the rest of the troop were out investigating the hiding-place of the robbers' loot, Dan rested in a comfortable chair by the fire. He was alone except for Gunticus, who was snoring gently in a corner, his precious jug clasped firmly in his arms. The boy had tried to express his gratitude for the part Gunticus had played in his rescue, but the old Indian had remained stolidly unconcerned. "You my friend," was all he would say.

From Ethan, Dan had learned more about it. Gunticus, on his way through the woods to the tavern that morning, had seen the snowshoe tracks and recognized them. Following the trail to the clearing he had found the shoes themselves in the edge of the brush-pile and had crawled in far enough to discover the hole where Dan had fallen through. On his return to the village nobody would pay any attention to him at first. The poor old man was never taken very seriously by the townspeople, and when he began jabbering in his broken gutturals they thought he was begging for a drink. At last he had made Ben Tucker listen to him. The blacksmith, it seemed, had been suspicious of the Nixons from the start. He had organized a party forthwith, and Dan knew the rest of the story.

At the end of half an hour the men came back into the kitchen through the trap-door. Tucker was rubbing his brawny hands with satisfaction.

"Plenty o' folks'll be glad to hear what we found back there," he said. "Must be two-three thousand dollars' worth o' stolen goods, not to speak o' the hosses an' rigs. Looks to me like this outfit belonged to the Stingers. Once we've got this nest cleaned out, though, they'll have a tough time startin' up in Deptford again!"

He turned to Tim Garrity. "Let's see, now, Tim," he remarked, "ain't I heard you brag about yer cookin'? How 'bout slingin' together an Irish stew fer the crowd? There's plenty o' vittles here an' we might as well make ourselves to home."

The hostler grinned. "Sure an' I'll fix up somethin' to make yer mouths water," he replied. "On'y I was thinkin' what a dither Skilly'll be in, wid nobody to help, whin the stage stops by!"

"Don't ye fret about Skilly," laughed his commanding officer. "This is Gover'ment business, ain't it? Capturin' mail robbers? An' by the way—mebbe I'd better take another look at that pair o' prisoners—make sure none o' the knots has slipped."

He descended through the trap-door again, and returned a few minutes later to report the captives securely tied.

Tim Garrity fully justified his reputation as a cook. When the big kettle of stew was ready, they all fell to with a will and made an excellent meal. Dan's weakness had passed and he was ravenously hungry. To him, at least, no banquet ever tasted more delicious.

"It's the onions," Tim confided to him afterward. "I 'most always put in double the onions of anny cook iver I heard of."

After the dishes were cleared away, there was nothing to do but wait. The horses had been fed and stabled, the tracks and blood-stains in the yard brushed over with clean snow, and now the little group sat quietly in the kitchen. The only light came from the fire and from a single candle that guttered in a bottle-neck on the table.

Outside, the night had shut down black and moonless, with a few stars glittering coldly overhead. Somewhere along the wooded roads to the north, Dan thought, a man would be riding now. Stealthily, like a hunted fox, slipping along through the shadows toward a lonely clearing in the woods.

The men around him in the room felt the tension as he did. When they spoke at all it was in whispers. They worked over their fire-arms, reloading them with care, putting fresh priming in the pans, polishing the barrels.

None of them had a watch and there was no clock in the house. The time seemed to drag endlessly. Garrity, who had once been a sailor, went to a window in one of the dark rooms, after a while. "About ten o'clock, I'd say, from the stars," he reported when he came back.

They continued to sit there in silence. Once 'Lije Hayes nodded off to sleep and had to be shaken awake. Every little while the wounded Joe Blake would try to find a more comfortable position on the bed where they had laid him and sigh a little with the pain. A fitful wind had risen outside. It whined and panted like an animal around the corners of the house.

Dan leaned over toward Tucker. "What became o' the dogs?" he whispered.

"Tim clubbed one of 'em, back o' the barn," he replied. "I guess t'other one run off into the woods."

"I was thinkin'," said Dan, "won't this feller think it's funny if there's no barkin'?"

The blacksmith nodded. "Can't be helped," he murmured. "I'm beginnin' to wonder if he's comin' at all."

Five minutes later Dan lifted a finger to his lips. "Listen!" he breathed. The sound he had heard came again—the deep-voiced, distant barking of a dog. Around the room there was a general shifting of cramped legs and arms.

"Think it's him?" Ethan whispered.

"Might be," said Ben Tucker softly. "Seems to be comin' closer. Anyhow, we may as well git ready. Everybody remember the orders. Dan, I don't want you mixed up in any rough work. Better go in the front room, hadn't ye?"

"Gosh, Ben—I'll be all right!" the boy pleaded. "Lemme stay here. I'll keep out o' the way."

"Well, git over there back o' the wood-box. Ethan, you're to open the door an' stay behind it. The rest of ye keep yer guns on him an' shoot if he makes a false move. Now douse that candle."

For the next few moments the only sound in the room was the crackle of the dying fire on the hearth. Then the intermittent barking of the dog ceased, and just outside, they heard the muffled trampling of a horse in the snow.

Dan held his breath. At last boots scraped lightly on the doorstep and knuckles rapped on the door. Once—twice—three times. Ethan started cautiously to lift the patched-up bar from its fastenings.

A voice spoke, low and sharp, outside. "Newt? Answer me!" Then, with a note of alarm—"Who's there, in the house?"

"Quick, boy—open it!" whispered Tucker. But before Ethan could pull the bar clear, they heard a sudden scramble on the steps. The blacksmith leaped forward, wrenching the door open by brute force. And against the snowy background of the clearing they caught a glimpse of a great black horse galloping away, with a dark-cloaked rider crouched low in the saddle.

Elijah Hayes was the first man through the doorway. He fired quickly but his rifle-ball went wide of the mark. The horse and rider disappeared in the darkness at the edge of the woods.

For a moment they stood there in stunned silence. Then Tim Garrity started for the stable with a yell.

"Where ye goin'?" roared Tucker. "Come back here. 'Fore ye could git a hoss saddled he'd be a mile off."

"Sure an' ain't we goin' to chase him, then?" returned the Irishman.

"Not now, we ain't. We're goin' to take our prisoners to the lock-up an' git Joe Blake home to a doctor. Mebbe in the mornin' we'll have a scheme to ketch this feller. Dan"—he turned to the boy—"did ye git a good look at the hoss he rode?"

"Yes," said Dan. "I saw him through the window here. 'Twas the same one—Cap'n Hairtrigger's hoss."

"Hm," the blacksmith frowned. "That's what I figgered. But what in 'tarnation scairt him off? Somethin' about the place must ha' looked wrong."

Dan's hand had been resting on the window-sill. He became conscious now of a roughness under his fingers. "Look!" he exclaimed. "It's candle-grease! A ring of it, right here on the ledge. Reckon they used to stick a candle here in the winder fer a signal?"

"Sure—that was the way of it!" Ethan put in. "There wouldn't be no other reason fer puttin' a candle over there."

"Looks like that was it," Tucker nodded. "Well, let's be goin'."

Grumbling over their failure, the men tramped out to

the stable and saddled their horses. The great square trap in the barn-floor was lifted and from the depths of the secret cellar they brought the little bay mare and Skilly Bassett's sleigh.

"If ye're feelin' enough better, Dan," the blacksmith told the boy, "ye better do the drivin' an' take Joe Blake in with ye. We'll tie the Nixons on their own hosses an' ride along behind."

The ride back to Deptford over the silent, deserted roads was like a dream to Dan. There was no talk or laughter among the tired men, and the horses moved quietly through the snow. In the village one or two lights still shone from the windows. Anxious wives and mothers were waiting up for their return.

Dan stopped at Joe Blake's house and helped the wounded trooper up the steps. "I'll try to get Doc Reynolds over here," he told Mrs. Blake. "Make him as comfortable as you can till I get back."

The doctor was in bed, but at Dan's urgent plea he dressed and accompanied the boy to Blake's. The outlaw's pistol-bullet had broken the collar-bone and glanced off without further damage, he found. The setting and bandaging were quickly done, but even so it was some time after midnight when Dan at last headed the mare up the hill.

There was still a light in the window of the keeping-room. As he drove up to the barn door Skilly Bassett rushed out, a greatcoat thrown over his woolen night-shirt and flapping around his bare shanks.

"She's here! By thunder she *is* here!" the inn-keeper cried ecstatically through chattering teeth. "Danny boy —I'm so tickled I could hug ye! Come on, Tim—git the mare in her stall an' put a blanket on her. Is she all right? She's all right, ain't she?"

His excited voice kept on all the time they were un-harnessing, rubbing the mare down and laying straw in her stall. Finally the hostler interrupted him. "Let's git to bed," he yawned. "I'm fair dead fer sleep, an' the lad here'll be faintin' away ag'in if ye kape him up much longer."

Gratefully, Dan saw them leave for the house. He spread his blanket in the hay and laid himself down. His tired brain whirled with pictures, terrifyingly distinct, of all he had been through in those last forty-eight hours. But it took only a few seconds for a healthy slumber to wipe them out.

.   .   .

Tim Garrity didn't wake him till broad daylight next morning. The inn-yard was noisy with men and horses.

"How d'ye feel now, lad?" asked the Irishman. "Ready to ride? Ben Tucker's here with the troop, an' we're startin' after that spalpeen that got away last night."

Dan got up as quickly as his stiff muscles would allow. He stretched himself and grinned. "Sure," he said. "I'm all right now—or will be if I can get some breakfast. What's the plan?"

Tim, who had already done the early stable chores, told him what was afoot as they went to the kitchen. "Ben's got old Gunticus sobered up, an' started him trailin' that black nag through the woods. Soon as the gang's rounded up, we'll ride over to the Half Moon road an' meet up wid the Injun. If he's as good a tracker as the boys say, he may be able to foller the trail even on the broken road an' find where it turns off. A slim chance, belikes, but Ben's set on recoverin' the money they stole."

Maria Bassett eyed the boy sharply as he came in. "Well," she said vehemently, "I never thought I'd see any o' *my* help lookin' as peaked as that! Set down quick, Dan, an' I'll make it up to ye fer the meals ye missed."

She was almost as good as her word. Hungry as he was, Dan had to give up before he had half finished the vast slabs of ham and stacks of buckwheat cakes she set before him.

It was close to ten o'clock before the last of the posse had assembled. Ben Tucker swung his big body into the saddle and waited a moment, looking around him sternly. There were twenty men and boys in the group. All were well armed and mounted on the best horses in the township.

"I've heard some o' ye sayin' we'd be foolish to go out again today," he said. "Ye think this robber's got too

much of a start on us. An' ye're saddle-sore now from ridin' 'round the country. I don't blame ye. But I'm tellin' ye, New Hampshiremen—an' 'specially Deptford men—don't quit that easy. We got two o' the three. Pease an' me worked on Newt Nixon all night after we got back, tryin' to make him turn state's evidence. He wouldn't crack. But here's why I figger we've got a chance to ketch the third one. Nixon kep' sayin' he'd be forty or fifty miles away by mornin'. He laid it on too thick—made sech a point of it that, by golly, I b'lieve he's hid out within a half a day's ride!

"Now don't fergit this. We're jest about certain this feller is Cap'n Hairtrigger—wanted in Boston, with a reward of a hundred dollars on his head. An' there'll be another reward if we git back the silver they took from the mail-stage. How much I can't tell ye, but it'll be a mighty good day's pay fer somebody. Now, save yer hosses all ye're able, an' obey orders. Come on!"

He wheeled his big gray saddle-horse and cantered out to the road with the troop streaming after him.

Dan and Ethan rode together near the end of the file of horsemen. The farm boy had brought along a mount for his friend—an easy-gaited chestnut mare with the chunky build and staying qualities of Morgan blood. "Paw said after what you'd been through, ye rated the best hoss in the barn," Ethan told him.

An hour's steady riding brought them to a point on the road to Half Moon Pond, some six miles north of the tavern. Coming over a rise, they saw a patient figure squatting beside the road, a little way ahead. Ben Tucker halted the posse. "There's Gunticus," he said. "You fellers stay here till I talk to him. If he's still on the trail, I don't want to spoil it with too many fresh tracks."

They waited only a moment or two. Then the blacksmith waved them forward.

"The man on the black hoss come out o' the woods a quarter of a mile ahead," he explained. "Turned left at first, to fool anybody that follered him—then come back this way, hidin' his tracks. Right here"—he pointed—"Gunticus says he jumped his hoss clean from the middle o' the road over the wall!"

The men murmured their amazement and unbelief. It was nearly five yards from the packed center of the road to the three-foot stone wall at the edge of the woods. The snow between was smooth and untrodden. Dan tried to picture the great black gathering those magnificent haunches under him and sailing arrow-like across the intervening space. He could only believe it because he had seen that horse in action. Even so it was almost incredible, for there had been no room for a running take-off.

Gunticus pointed in silence to a pair of deep cuts in the packed road, where the toe-calks of the hind feet had taken hold. Then he indicated a place where loose snow had been dislodged from the top of the wall.

They rode their horses nearer and saw the tracks on the other side that left no room for doubt.

"All right," said Tucker. "Git yer guns primed an' ready. It may not be much further. Gunticus, come up here with me if ye want. We oughta be able to foller this trail from hoss-back."

The Indian shook his head. "No," he grunted. "You ride. Me run." And so saying he jogged ahead on his snowshoes, bent far forward like an old hound nosing a rabbit-track.

They followed in single file. Dan's mare had fallen in just behind the blacksmith's big gray, so that most of the time he was able to see the Indian's bowed figure. The woods were thick and he had to crouch low in his saddle, throwing up an arm to fend off the branches that whipped across his face. They had progressed in this way for more than two miles when Gunticus paused, holding up his hand. The trail of the black horse had joined another trail, marked by many hooves, which bore off a little to the right."

"We findum pretty quick," said the Indian, laconically. "Mebbe hide in Injun cave, top of hill."

Quietly, Ben Tucker called the troop together and told them where Gunticus thought the outlaw might be concealed. "Spread out, now," he ordered. "Ninety or a hundred foot apart, so we'll cover three sides o' the hill. When ye've had time to git in position, we'll all start ridin' towards the top. If he comes out, don't stop to argue—shoot. If he's in the cave an' stays there, we'll have him trapped."

Dan and Ethan moved out toward the left-hand wing of the fan. The slope ahead of them was not only thickly wooded but strewn with huge boulders and ledges, some of them half as big as a house. There was no signal given, but Dan caught a glimpse of the rider next to him starting to move up the hill, and he clucked softly to the mare. She climbed at a quick walk, picking her way among the rocks and trees.

They had covered nearly half the distance to the hill-top when the silence of their advance was suddenly broken. Far over at the other end of the line a horse whinnied loudly. Dan heard a crackling of brush as other troopers pushed forward in haste. He dug the mare's ribs with his boot-heel. Right in front of him rose a crag of granite a dozen feet high, and he guided his mount around it to the left. As the good beast scrambled upward there came a yell that froze his blood. Quick hooves were pounding on the hillside above. Then, through the screening hemlock boughs, he caught sight of something big and black charging down like an avalanche. The rider must have glimpsed him at the same instant, for the black horse swerved, heading straight for the top of the high ledge.

Paralyzed with horror, Dan saw the man's white face —the hands pulling desperately at the bridle-reins—the frenzied effort of the horse to check itself in time. Then they were hurtling over the cliff's edge. And as he jerked the mare around, the boy heard the muffled crash of their fall.

The sight that met his eyes a moment later made him physically sick. The gleaming body of the great black

THEY WERE HURTLING OVER THE CLIFF

horse lay among the snowy rocks, quivering in the agony of death. Its neck had been broken in the plunge. And a dozen feet away, the twisted shape of a man was sprawled.

Dan dismounted shakily. He saw the man's face move —turn toward him. He had his musket ready but before he had taken two steps nearer, he knew no weapon would be needed. There was a strange look in those pale gray eyes. A surprised look, almost wistful.

The thin lips forced themselves into a smile, and with an effort the man spoke. "We meet—again—Master Drew," came the gasping voice. "Fate seems to—bring us together—in odd places."

TWENTY

SO startled was Dan at hearing his name spoken, he could only stare at the injured outlaw. There was no doubt left in his mind about the man's identity. The same pale, piercing eyes had looked into his the night he came to Deptford. But how could the "Mr. Lamb" of that encounter know anything at all about him—Dan Drew?

"Why do you—stand there looking at me, boy?" came the ghost of a voice again. "The money's in those saddle-bags. It's silver, boy—heavy." He caught his breath painfully. "Too heavy!" he sighed.

The boy wrenched his eyes away from that tortured smile and shouted at the top of his lungs. "Ben—Ben Tucker! Here he is!"

The look on the man's face was more than he could stand. He turned aside quickly, walking toward the body of the horse. Tied to the saddle-cantle were two big leather pouches, sagging with the weight of silver they contained. Too heavy! Without those added pounds—who could tell? Perhaps the great black brute might have made his leap in safety.

Shouts came through the trees. Other members of the posse had heard his call and were hurrying to join him. He saw Ethan—Tim Garrity—Ben Tucker—crashing through the hemlock brush.

"Where is he?" bellowed the blacksmith. The gray horse he rode halted suddenly, snorting and rearing. Almost under its feet was the limp, still body of the highwayman.

Tucker swung down from the saddle. "Is he dead?" he asked soberly. Before Dan found words to answer, the smith was kneeling in the snow. "Tim," he said quickly, "fetch me the flask of brandy from my saddle-pocket."

He took the leathern bottle from the hostler and put it to the outlaw's lips. One by one, the troopers dismounted. They came to stand in an awkward ring about the pair on the ground. It was so quiet that for the first time Dan could hear the soft *hush-hush* of the wind in the hemlock-tops.

Then the faint voice was speaking again.

"Could you—lift me up a little? Thanks. It's the spine—seventh vertebra, I believe. Yes, gentlemen—I've no illusions. I am a dying man."

In the pause that followed he seemed to be struggling

for breath. At last he went on, speaking in a whisper that was broken by painful silences.

"Some of you have known me under various names," he said. "My true name is Michael O'Hara, and I was born in Irish County Clare. Eight years ago I left Dublin University with my degree in medicine. And because the openings for a young doctor were few at home, I took ship for the colony of Barbados. It was there, when I had established a successful practice, that I met the daughter of a Spanish planter. . . . She was young and talented and very beautiful . . ."

His voice trailed off, and for a moment he lay quiet, mustering his ebbing strength. When he resumed they had to bend close to catch his words.

"I must tell you these things," he said, "while life is in me . . . so that perhaps you may understand. . . .

"Her family was proud. They resented my attentions. I quarreled with her brother and killed him in a duel. . . . It became necessary for me to flee for my life, and the girl chose to accompany me. When we landed in Baltimore we were married. . . .

"Again I tried to practice medicine, but the rumors that had followed me from the islands made it impossible. There were days when we had no food, no lodging. . . . Desperate, I walked the dark streets and haunted the taverns. And one night I robbed a drunken man of his money. . . . After that, my wife was never again in want. . . ."

Panting weakly, he closed his eyes for a little space. When he began to speak once more, the terrible smile

was wrenching at his lips. "It was then that the career of the great Captain Hairtrigger began. In Maryland and Pennsylvania, in Connecticut and Massachusetts, that name became a word to frighten children. . . . I soon had friends in many states and traveled as I pleased from one adventure to another. Three years ago our little daughter was born. I saw her only rarely. My wife never knew what the business was that kept me so much away from home. But she had a comfortable house—

servants—carriages—and her life centered in the child, Dolores. . . ."

At the name, a stir went through the quiet circle of men. A look of understanding passed from one to another.

"Something—I shall never know what—made my wife unhappy. In November she set out to find me. You know the sad ending of that journey. . . . I resolved to gain possession of my child—to get together what money I could—and to return with her to Ireland. For that purpose I put on once more the guise of a medico. Yes—I was that Dr. Barlow who spent some time at your village inn. . . ."

After a grim effort he went on, weak and gasping. "The game—is up. I am a doctor and I know. I ask no mercy—for myself. But, gentlemen—for my—little girl . . ."

A fit of choking contorted his white face. His body seemed to shrink and sag. Hastily Ben Tucker lifted the brandy flask to his mouth again, but the outlaw made no attempt to swallow. His head fell back across the smith's supporting arm, and under the locks of black hair they could see the scar of the brand on his forehead.

After a moment Ben laid him gently in the snow. "All over," he said in a husky voice.

.   .   .   .

They buried Michael O'Hara in the Deptford churchyard two days later. He was laid to rest by the side of his wife—that lovely, tragic lady who had left her island home for him and perished in a northern blizzard.

The two Nixons were held in jail for the spring session of court, and for weeks after their capture men were coming from far and near to prove ownership of the stolen goods found in the dug-out under the barn.

Gradually affairs in the village settled back into their quiet routine. The vigilance committee was mustered out, its services no longer needed. And up at the tavern on the hill, business went forward as usual.

Dan welcomed the peaceful round of activities. The rising at cock-crow to groom and harness the stage horses; the stable chores; the warm welcome of the inn-kitchen; and the evenings when tall stories and mugs of ale and cider passed from man to man around the hearth in the keeping-room.

In late February the pod-auger sleds became less numerous on the road. The farmers were at home getting ready for spring sugar-making. Outside of the regular visits of the stages few travelers stopped at the Fox and Stars. However, another interest had come to occupy the community. Public notices were posted, advertising the sale at auction of the Caleb Wentworth place, across the road from Hayes'. It was known throughout the district as a good farm. The stones were well cleared, the buildings roomy and stoutly timbered. There were a hundred acres of pasture and woodland and eighty more of fertile intervale along the river. A dozen good dairy cattle and sixty sheep went with the property.

Caleb Wentworth had died during the winter and his wife was disposing of the farm so that she might move to Keene and live with her sister.

There was lively speculation at the tavern as to the purchaser. Most people thought it would be Squire Pierce, who had plenty of money and liked to turn a trade in farmland when he could buy it at his own figure. Nobody else in Deptford seemed likely to give him any opposition.

Ethan was glum when he came over to see Dan, a few days before the sale. "Durn old skin-flint!" he grumbled. "What's he need of it? Right there so close to us, it means somethin' to have good neighbors. Reckon Paw'd buy it himself if he had the cash—jest to keep the squire from gittin' hold of it! We don't have no need fer more land, but that's a mighty good farm fer somebody."

The day of the auction dawned fair and mild. For the first time there was a promise of coming spring in the air. A soft south wind blew damply over the snow-crust and water ran in chuckling rivulets along the roadside ditches.

"Suttinly feels like a thaw," said Skilly Bassett, coming out to the barn where Dan was at work. "The damp's made my rheumatiz worse. Got it so bad in my right arm I can't hardly lift it. Still—I don't want to miss the Wentworth sale. Guess mebbe I'll let ye drive me over."

"Yes, sir!" replied Dan, trying to hide his eagerness.

"Hmm—I thought so," nodded the inn-keeper. "Jest like a boy—anxious to go gallivantin'. Well, I don't see's it can be helped this time. Git the mare ready an' we'll start in half an hour."

There were more than a score of sleighs and pungs at the Wentworth farm when they drove up, and new ones were arriving every few moments. By the time the scheduled hour of the sale approached there must have been a crowd of close to two hundred men milling about in the slush in front of the house door.

The auctioneer was none other than Noah Winslow, who owned the gristmill in Deptford. He was known throughout the county for his loud voice and jocular manner, and if anybody could get a fair price for an article, he could. It was told of him that he had once auctioned off a broken ox-yoke and four sap buckets to a spinster lady who lived in town and took in sewing.

Winslow had set up his little table on the doorstep. He looked around to see if there were any more late-comers, glanced importantly at his watch, and hit the table a resounding blow with his wooden hammer.

"All right, folks," he called cheerfully. "Reckon ye all know what we're here for. This property, which I may safely say is one o' the two finest farms in the whole Contoocook valley—"

He paused rhetorically and someone brought a laugh by asking who owned the other one.

"I won't name the other one, but I reckon each one of ye has his own idee," chuckled Winslow. "Now this extry fine farm," he went on, "is to be sold today to the highest bidder. One hundred an' eighty acres o' the fairest soil the sun of New Hampshire shines upon! Most of ye know the buildin's. They're solid-built an' snug. There's twelve head o' good milch cattle in the barn—two of 'em due to freshen next month—an' eight ton o' clover hay to feed 'em. There's as well-conditioned a flock o' sheep as you'll find in Dep'ford township. There's ten acres o' new orchard. All five- an' six-year-old trees—sops-o'-wines an' russets. There's farm tools, plows, harrers an' wagons. Everything on the place goes in one passel, exceptin' the furniture, the hoss, an' one kerridge.

"Now, folks! What am I offered? Lemme hear an

openin' bid. Lemme hear a figger that shows some real appreciation o' this magnificent opportunity!"

The assembled farmers shifted their feet and grinned, waiting.

"Fifteen hundred," said Squire Pierce, carelessly. Dan, wedged in beside Ethan Hayes in the front row, craned his neck till he could see the village potentate. There was studied indifference on his heavy-jowled face.

"You've heard the bid," bawled the auctioneer. "Fifteen hundred dollars fer a farm wuth four times that! Now let's git down to serious business. Who'll say two thousand?"

Someone else offered sixteen hundred, a third man sixteen-fifty, and the squire jumped it to two thousand. From there, the bidding went up by hundreds and fifties, slowing a little as it reached three thousand dollars.

"Thirty-five hundred!" came a deep voice from the back of the crowd.

Squire Pierce's face reddened and he looked around with a frown. "Thirty-six," he snapped.

"Thirty-seven hundred," the answer was promptly returned. The squire seemed perturbed. He took a paper from his pocket and did some calculating, while the auctioneer continued to plead for more bids. The rest of the neighbors had shut up in the face of this new competition.

"Who is that other feller?" Ethan whispered glee-fully. "He's makin' the squire sweat a little!"

"I can't see him from here," Dan returned. "An' I can't seem to place his voice. Must be a stranger."

Finally Squire Pierce cleared his throat portentously and held up a fat hand. "I offer four thousand dollars!" he announced in truculent tones.

There was a deal of staring and low-voiced talk among the expectant crowd. Ethan shook his head dole-fully. "Reckon that settles it," he murmured. "That's more'n most folks has got."

"I'm offered four thousand," droned the auctioneer, his keen eyes searching the throng. "Four thousand—who'll gimme forty-one—make it forty-one—forty I got—do I hear forty-one—"

"Forty-one hundred," said the deep-voiced man at the rear.

"Forty-two!" the squire roared, puffing up like a turkey gobbler.

"Forty-three," was the firm reply.

Squire Pierce made as if to speak again, then checked himself. "Hunh!" he muttered uncertainly. "I don't want the durn place anyhow. Why, 'tain't actually worth more'n six thousand—"

The men nearest him burst into laughter and the squire turned angrily to walk away. Winslow lifted his hammer.

"Ye've heard the bid, folks," he chanted. "Goin'—at forty-three hundred. Anybody raise it? Make it forty-four? Do I hear forty-four? Goin'—fer the last time at forty-three! Goin'—" he waited—"goin'—an'—*gone* to the tall feller in the fur cap at forty-three hundred dollars. How d'ye want to settle fer it, Mister?"

"Cash, I reckon," the successful bidder answered. And as the crowd separated to let him through, Dan caught a glimpse of a big figure in bearskin coat and cap. Then he saw the weathered brown face and gave a sudden start. "Look!" he cried, seizing Ethan's arm. "It's Silas Penny!" And he rushed forward to greet his old friend of the road.

TWENTY-ONE

THE big wagon-freighter was standing in front of the auctioneer's table, counting out bills from a capacious wallet. "I b'lieve that does it," he said, laying down the final greenback. "I wouldn't ha' wanted to travel with so much money on me if I hadn't heard how you folks had smoked out the Stingers."

He turned as the boy approached. "Well, I snum! Dan Drew!" he cried heartily. "Jest the feller I wanted to see. Is Skilly here with ye? 'Cause him an' you an' me have got some business to talk over."

They shook hands, and Dan looked around to find Skilly Bassett at his elbow. "Yes, sirree!" said the innkeeper. "I'm here, all right, an' I kin sort o' suspicion what ye want to talk about. Glad you're goin' to be a neighbor, Silas, even if I lose money by it. Your board an' lodgin' used to come to quite a figger in the course of a year!"

Before the crowd had time to disperse, Winslow banged the table again and cupped his hands to shout.

"Hold on, everybody!" he bellowed. "The Selectmen asked me to tell ye there's a special session o' Town Meetin' called fer tonight. Asa Pease has got a mighty important piece o' business to decide, an' ye'll be sorry afterwards if ye ain't there to vote. That's all. See ye at the town hall after supper!"

Dan got into the cutter beside his employer, and guided the mare into the procession of sleighs and saddle-horses that was moving village-ward. Just behind them was Silas Penny, driving one of his big red roan pullers. "I don't expect to keep up with ye," he called, "but I'll be at the tavern fer dinner."

Lady was eager to go. As the road widened a little, Skilly grinned at his young driver. "All right," he said, "let her out a bit."

Dan slacked the reins and clucked softly, and the mare shot out to the left around the next two sleighs. There was a gap of fifty yards in front of them now, and up in the lead was a single cutter—Squire Pierce with his fast chestnut road-horse, Ginger. The highway was smooth and well-packed from there into Deptford, half a mile away.

The Lady mare cleared her nostrils with a business-like snort, and stretched her slim legs smoothly. She had caught the spirit of the chase. Her head was thrust out and her ears cocked forward. Faster and faster her hooves beat their tattoo on the hard snow.

The squire threw a quick glance over his shoulder and leaned forward, reaching for the whip.

"Watch him!" Skilly chuckled. "He's took one beatin' today, an' he hates to be licked wuss'n pizen!"

Under the touch of the whip the chestnut started to trot in earnest. They were only twenty yards behind now, but the gap between the sleighs became no shorter. Skilly watched Dan's hands on the reins.

"You're a natchal good driver," he said, "but she likes to hear me talk to her. Come on now, Gal—*tch, tch*— you can do better'n that! Pick 'em up a leetle faster, now—that's the way!"

His voice was soft and wheedling, entirely different from his usual sour tone. The mare put one ear back, then flicked it forward again. Without any noticeable effort her speed seemed to double. As the spire of Deptford Church appeared over the hill, they drew up within a few feet of the cutter ahead.

"This ain't no place to try to pass," Skilly murmured. "Keep her as she is till we're down on the level again."

Both horses slowed a trifle to keep their footing on the down-grade. They were in the outskirts of the village now. A housewife in a dust-cap thrust her head out of a doorway and waved her broom excitedly as they flashed by.

"Now!" breathed Skilly. "Git the whip ready, an' jest trail it over her back."

Dan gathered the reins and tickled the shining bay flank with the tassel of the driving-whip. At the touch the mare almost jerked the cutter from under them. He pulled her head to the left just in time, skimming so close to the other sleigh that Squire Pierce must have felt her hot breath on his neck.

They went by in a cloud of flying snow and led the fast-trotting chestnut into Deptford Four Corners by a length. Skilly turned and waved his good arm in farewell, as the disgruntled squire drove toward his own house on Main Street.

.   .   .   .   .   .

It was after they had eaten one of Maria Bassett's best dinners that the landlord called Dan into the keeping-room. Silas Penny was already seated by the fire, shaving a plug of tobacco for his long clay pipe.

"Well," said Skilly, "here's the boy. I guess ye kin fire away now, Silas."

The big wagoner picked up a red ember in the tongs and lighted up. After a few thoughtful puffs, he began speaking. "The wife an' me have been plannin' fer years that I'd quit haulin' an' settle down on a farm," he said. "I've done well—reckon I've saved all I need to live comfortable. So when Nate Gilman brought word o' this sale I got my money together an' drove on down. Freightin' over the roads, I've seen every town 'twixt the Connecticut an' the sea, an' there ain't a place I'd sooner live in than Dep'ford. I understand Mis' Wentworth'll be moved out in a couple more weeks, so we'll be able to git settled 'fore frost is out o' the ground. I'm jest itchin' to see that big wheel-team o' mine pullin' a plow."

He paused a moment, then looked at Dan. "I reckon you've been pretty happy here?" he asked.

Dan nodded, wondering.

"Ye see"—Silas hesitated—"the Missus an' me sort o' figger we might be lonesome up there on the farm with no chick nor child. I'd like a good stout boy to help around the place an' be kind of a son to us. But if Skilly needs ye—"

The landlord made a loud clatter among the glasses on the bar. "I reckon we could spare him," he said gruffly. "He's earned his keep, but Tim an' me got along well enough without no help in years past. The young 'un's smart. He oughta be goin' to school, an' he can't do that whilst he's workin' here."

There was a long silence when he finished speaking. On the hearth a log fell with a sudden crackle, sending up a shower of sparks into the wide throat of the chimney.

"Well, Danny?" asked Silas Penny quietly.

Dan couldn't speak for a minute. He had a choking feeling in his throat. There had been so little kindness in his life that the homely good-will of these two men touched him almost to tears.

His voice came huskily at last. "Golly, Silas," he said, "I can't think of anythin' I'd rather do than come to live with you! But"—he turned toward Skilly—"you've been awful good to me—you an' Mrs. Bassett. I hate to leave here, an' I'll do whatever you say."

The landlord broke the tension with a friendly laugh. "You go right ahead, youngster! 'Tain't as if ye was movin' to Chiny. We'll still see plenty of ye, I reckon! Now skip out to the barn an' give Tim a hand with the chores. The down stage is due in twenty minutes."

.   .   .

By seven o'clock that night half the people in Deptford township were assembled in the big, raftered room
above the general store. Squire Pierce, Amos Crandall,
Ben Tucker and the other Selectmen sat on a low platform facing the packed crowd. When the squire had
called the meeting to order, Asa Pease got up to speak.
The fat little constable's high-pitched voice rang loud
in the attentive silence.

"Three weeks ago," he announced, "I sent off letters
an' affidavits to the Danvers Thief Detectin' Society,
an' the Mariners' Bank. I give 'em the facts about our
capturin' the outlaw known as Cap'n Hairtrigger, an'
recoverin' the bank's money, stole from the mail-stage.
Now I got answers to both letters."

He paused dramatically. "There's a hundred dollars
reward from each one of 'em," he went on. "An' the
business before this meetin' is to decide who gits the
two rewards!"

There was a buzz of excited comment in every corner
of the hall. After a moment someone called out, "Let's
hear from Ben Tucker! He was leader o' the posse."

The blacksmith got up slowly, hunching his broad
shoulders. "Well, folks," he began, "it's a fact I oughta
be able to jedge. I was on the spot, an' I reckon the rest
o' the troop'll back up what I say. It's my opinion we
never would ha' caught up with O'Hara, or found the

cash either, if it hadn't been fer two people. One of em's the Injun, Gunticus. He's the only man in the township that could have follered that trail. My vote fer the first reward goes to Gunticus."

Several people voiced their disagreement. The Indian, they claimed, was a town charge and incapable of taking care of the money.

"What's the matter with givin' it to young Dan Drew?" one taxpayer asked. "He made the real capture, didn't he?"

Dan, sitting near the back of the hall with Skilly and Silas, got to his feet, trembling.

"I'd like to say somethin'," he spoke up. "Most likely I wouldn't ha' been here now if Gunticus hadn't found my tracks an' got Ben Tucker to bring the troop. He saved my life. An' afterwards he led us right up to the cave where the cap'n was hidin'. If anybody deserves it, Gunticus does."

Applause greeted his remarks, and on the vote that followed the "Ayes" carried the motion almost unanimously.

The blacksmith stood up again. "Now," his voice rumbled above the chatter, "let's talk about that second reward. I don't believe there's a man or woman here that won't agree where that oughta go. The feller I mean was ridin' the stage when the hold-up happened.

He put up a good scrap against odds. He was the first to find who the outlaws were, an' he suffered fer it a-plenty. Then he give us the tip that the third man we wanted was comin' back, an' we mighty nigh nabbed him that night. Next day, he was the first one to see Hairtrigger fall, an' the first to find the silver in the saddle-bags. He ain't lived amongst us very long, but I fer one'll say he's as good a Dep'ford man as anybody in this room. Ye all know who I mean. Dan Drew!"

A roar went up that shook the building. "Bring him up here!" Tucker beckoned, and Silas Penny swung the protesting boy to his shoulder, pushing his way forward through the crowd. Other bearers joined them as they advanced, and by the time they reached the platform Dan was hoisted high aloft by a dozen strong arms.

The meeting cheered and cheered again. "Speech! We want a speech!" came the cry from various quarters of the hall. But Ben Tucker held up a huge hand for silence. "That ain't fair," he said, when order had been restored. "We all know Dan's happy to have us feel this way about him. No use makin' him miserable by askin' him to talk. When I was his age I'd ruther take a lickin' any day than make a speech, an' I reckon all boys is the same. But, Dan, lad—we're proud to hev ye fer a citizen! Give him the money, Asa. This don't need no vote!"

Dan walked back to the tavern with Silas Penny, his heart too full for talk. A big yellow moon was coming up over the eastern hills, making a shining pathway across the fields. The whole valley seemed alive with tiny voices—the gurgle of a thousand rills of water, singing under the snow—the muted jingle of home-going sleighbells—the rustle of bare twigs in the warm spring wind.

The man and the boy stopped a moment under the creaking sign of the Fox and Stars, looking back across the river.

"Mighty pretty night," said Silas, and Dan nodded. He was thinking beyond this night to the coming summer, and the joy of working on the farm with the big roan team. After that would come winter, and he would be going to school along with Ethan and Molly Crandall. And on ahead stretched the good years of growing up—taking his man's place in this pleasant village where he had found respect and friendship and a home.

"Yes, *sir!*" he answered. "It's a *mighty* pretty night!"

THE END